HERO ON A BICYCLE

HERO ON A BICYCLE

A NOVEL BY

Shirley Hughes

WALKER
BOOKS

First published 2012 by Walker Books Ltd
87 Vauxhall Walk, London SE11 5HJ

2 4 6 8 10 9 7 5 3 1

Text © 2012 Shirley Hughes
Cover photograph © 2012 Andreas Kuehn/Taxi/Getty Images
Interior illustrations and map © 2012 Shirley Hughes
Research by Jack Owen

This book has been typeset in Times

Printed and bound in Great Britain by Clays Ltd, St Ives plc

British Library Cataloguing in Publication Data:
a catalogue record for this book is available from the British Library

ISBN 978-1-4063-3611-5

www.walker.co.uk
www.heroonabicycle.co.uk

For Emma Curzon and Jack Owen,
without whose invaluable help and encouragement
this book would never have been written

FOREWORD

I always knew I would write this story one day.

I was nineteen when I first saw Florence and I thought it was the most beautiful city I had ever seen. I had my sketchbook with me and I was enchanted by the narrow winding streets, the washing hanging out of the shuttered windows and the sun-bleached ochres and terracotta browns of the roofs and walls, as well as the grand architecture.

This was not long after the end of the Second World War – the time in which *Hero on a Bicycle* is set. Although Florence had been miraculously spared the devastation which had been visited on many European cities during that war, there was a lot of poverty and food was still scarce for those who could not afford to buy on the black market. Tourists were beginning to trickle back, even though many streets still bore the marks of military occupation. So when I came to write this story, it was easy for me to imagine what the Italian people went through in wartime – when Hitler's Nazi army was fighting the Allies on Italian soil after Italy's own strutting dictator, Benito Mussolini, whom they had followed with such fervour, had so miserably let them down.

On Sunday mornings the ex-Partisans used to gather in the Piazza Goldoni, which was near to where I was living. They had been anti-Fascist freedom fighters during the war and some still sported their red bandanas around their necks to show their Communist allegiance. Although they no longer carried rifles, they still sang their old marching songs while brandishing clenched fists. They were recalling the time when they had roamed the hills around Florence, hampering German troop movements by blowing up bridges and railway lines and helping escaped Allied prisoners of war to rejoin their units. If they were caught by the dreaded German secret police, the Gestapo, it meant torture and execution. When, in 1944, the British and Canadian troops at last entered Florence, the Partisans came out of hiding and joined in the bitter fighting as, street by street, the city was liberated. After it was over, they meted out pitiless revenge upon anyone who had collaborated with the Fascists.

My fictional thirteen-year-old "hero on a bicycle", Paolo Crivelli, is living with his mother and older sister, Constanza, in their home in the hills outside the city of Florence during that summer of 1944, just as the Allied advance is approaching. Paolo and Constanza's father, Franco, – a passionate anti-Fascist – is in hiding and none of them know where. Their story was inspired by a courageous family I got to know on that first visit to Florence at the end of the war. The children, like Paolo and Constanza, had an English mother who was persuaded by the Partisans to help escaping prisoners of war. It was a very risky undertaking as it was punishable by death.

Paolo and Constanza are two young people who find themselves caught up in extraordinary and often terrifying circumstances that demand all their courage. But, like all teenagers, they still hang on to their dreams.

This is my first novel and also the first book I have

ever attempted without doing my own illustrations. Luckily for me, it is now possible for young readers to access evocative visual background information on the Internet: contemporary newsreels and photographs of Second World War aircraft tanks and weaponry, along with images of Partisans and armies on the march and refugees fleeing the bombing, as well as material from my sketchbooks, fashion drawings and hit songs of the era can all be found online at: www.heroonabicycle.co.uk.

Shirley Hughes

CHAPTER 1

When Paolo reached the deserted stretch of road where it was too steep to pedal he dismounted and began to wheel his bicycle instead. He knew it was far too late for him to be out. He was not supposed to go out alone after dark at all and so, inevitably, it was something he spent a good deal of his time plotting to do. It was around two o'clock in the morning and the high walls on either side of the road gave his footsteps a curious double echo; it was, as always, frightening.

His way ahead lay uphill. He was returning home from one of his secret night rides into Florence, which now lay behind him in its bowl of hills, a dark, closely shuttered wartime city. There was very little traffic except for police and army trucks at that time of night. Streets and squares were dark and silent, and the bridges that spanned the silvery, snaking River Arno were all unlit. If he looked back he could see the familiar ribbed dome of the cathedral and its attendant bell tower, which he had known since childhood, flattened against the silhouette of the northern suburbs. By day they were part of his ordinary world. At this time of night they were not so reassuring.

The houses on either side of the road were mostly large nineteenth-century mansions, set well apart and looming in spacious gardens behind locked iron gates. Many of them were now closed up. Their owners had abandoned them and decamped to the countryside, where food was less scarce. No hospitable light spilled onto the road and only dry leaves skittered across the fitful beam of his carefully shaded bicycle lamp. He began to wonder why he did this. The most exciting part, really, was planning his escape – the elaborate subterfuge of pretending to go to bed early and listening out for his mother's footsteps on the stairs and her heels tapping along the side landing and then waiting for her to say her last prayers of the day and turn out her light. Then came his own noiseless descent, the squeeze through the back pantry window and the agonizing tension of trying to remove his bicycle from the shed without disturbing his old dog, Guido. Maria, the only servant who still "lived in", occupied the room behind the kitchen, but she slept like a log. His older sister Constanza's bedroom was on the top floor, and it was a fairly safe bet that if she did hear anything she would not bother to let on.

The climax of the escapade was the moment when he took off all alone, freewheeling downhill in the dark with a fresh wind in his face. And it was over much too soon. Escape was essential, though. He had to get away from the boredom, the pinched wartime austerities of his home: Constanza's tiresome aloofness, his mother's goodness and the burden of endlessly being expected to be helpful. With his father away, a household of women – relieved only by the coming and going of priests, who did not count as men – was no place for him.

The city at night fascinated him. At thirteen, he liked to think he was one of those characters who welcomed the darkness to pursue their own particular purposes, like his current hero, James Cagney, whom he had seen in American movies: hard-boiled, not always on the right side of the law and devastatingly attractive to women in spite of being short and not very handsome. With these thoughts in his head, Paolo would cycle along streets of shops that were familiar by day but now mysterious, with all their shutters down. Sometimes he would catch a glimpse of lovers in shadowed doorways. He had learned how to dodge drunks and gangs of boys much tougher than he was and to dismount and whisk around corners to avoid the civil or military police, and to keep well within the shadow of the wall in deserted squares. The huddled groups he sometimes came upon, deeply immersed in murmured conversation, cigarettes aglow in the dark and faces theatrically lit for a second by the flare of a match, excited him deeply. So, most of all, did those side streets where doors opened and closed briefly to reveal dimly lit interiors inhabited, so Maria said, by "bad women".

But, beginning to trudge home in the small hours of the morning, he felt the usual sense of anti-climax and frustration. Nothing had happened, and now he had to face the anxiety of getting back into the house again without being discovered.

He stopped and slung his bicycle against a nearby wall to get his breath back and consider the situation. At that moment someone came up silently behind him and clapped a strong hand over his mouth.

CHAPTER 2

"*Silenzio!* Don't try to struggle," said a man's voice close to his ear. No chance of that. Paolo felt himself go limp with fear. His first thought was that he might have wet himself and he prayed that it was not enough to notice. His next thought was: *I'm going to be beaten up*. His arms were jerked behind his back and pinioned. Whoever it was – and he sensed there were two of them – they were much bigger than he was. He was swung round and the hand was removed from his mouth. He screwed up his face, but no blow came.

In front of him was a man who, he guessed, was smaller than the one who was still gripping his hands tightly behind his back. The man wore a peaked cap pulled well down and a scarf pulled well up over the lower part of his face. His deep-set, slightly slanting eyes glittered in the dark – eyes like a fox's. He had a shotgun, but it was not pointed at Paolo. Instead, he held it nonchalantly in the crook of his arm like a man out shooting birds. *But I bet it's loaded,* thought Paolo.

"You – Paolo Crivelli?"

Paolo nodded. *How do you know my name?* he wanted to ask, but his mouth was too dry to speak.

"*Attenzione* – listen carefully. We're not going to hurt you if you know how to keep quiet, understood?" The man who held him jerked Paolo's neck backwards as though to emphasize this point.

"You're *Signora* Crivelli's son?"

Another nod.

"We have a message for your mother."

My mother? Paolo turned completely cold with terror. What could men like these want with his mother?

"We need to speak with her. Not at the house. Wait till you're alone with her and then tell her we're in the area and we'll be getting in touch – tomorrow night if we can – the usual way."

Paolo said nothing.

"Do like we tell you. And if anyone else – *anyone*, understand? – finds out and sticks their nose in, it'll be her that gets trouble."

The grip on Paolo's arms tightened. Paolo nodded again. Then, quite suddenly, he was let go. The man who had held him spun him around to face the way home, picked up his bicycle and thrust it at him.

"Get going," he said, giving him a shove.

Without a word, Paolo mounted his bike and forced his trembling legs to carry him away up the hill. He did not look back; he knew that if he did, the road behind him would already be empty.

He was still numb with shock when he reached home. He badly wanted to be sick, but first he had to stop his old dog, Guido, from barking. He had remembered to bring a piece of ham bone in his pocket for the purpose. As a guard dog, Guido was a complete failure. He had never been much good at it and now in old age he had more or less given up trying, but that didn't stop him from barking. Before the war, Paolo's father had had three dogs besides Guido: two fine hunting dogs and another watchdog. But now he had gone away, the family were left with only Guido, and there was hardly enough food even for him.

Guido lay chained up in his kennel, dozing. When he heard Paolo coming he got up, stiff-legged, and came out stretching his front paws and making half-hearted growling noises. Paolo produced the ham bone and the dog snaffled it eagerly, then settled down to gnaw it with what remained of his back teeth. Paolo wheeled his bicycle on towards the house, past the barn and the outhouses, and propped it up against the wall next to Maria's, a high, old-fashioned model with two big baskets before and behind. Then he swung himself up onto the lower part of the shed roof.

Now for the pantry window. He climbed up to where he had escaped from earlier in the night. He had left the window propped open with a bit of stick, the gap just wide enough for him to get back in again. But, fumbling with exhaustion as he was, he managed to knock the stick and the window slammed shut. There was no outside catch.

Paolo laid his head down for a moment on the shed roof. He felt too tired to move. *Now,* he thought, *I'll have to stay out here until morning, or else knock up the family to let me in. And that means no more night rides. Ever.*

It was some time before he remembered the old trapdoor. It was at the side of the house, set in the ground of what had once been a paved yard. The door was invisible now because it was overgrown with weeds. In the past it had been used to lower casks of wine and olive oil into a storage space off the main cellar, but that was a long time ago. *Will it still open?* he wondered. *Worth a try, perhaps?*

He braced himself and slid down from the roof as silently as he could. He found the spot and began pulling away tangled ivy and stinging nettles. It was painfully hard work. At last he uncovered a rusty iron ring and pulled on it as hard as he could. The trapdoor creaked open, revealing a rotting wooden ladder that led down into pitch darkness. Gingerly, he lowered himself onto the first rung, tried its strength and descended. Halfway down, one rung abruptly gave way under him. He managed to slither the rest of the way down, grazing his hands badly but landing on his feet.

The storage cellar was a windowless, low-ceilinged space, reeking of damp and decay and ventilated only by a small grating. *If only I'd been sensible enough to bring my bicycle lamp,* thought Paolo, but it was too late now.

He knew a small door in the wall led into the main storage cellar under the house. Cautiously, he groped his way along one slimy wall, half expecting a bony hand to shoot out of the darkness and fasten on his wrist. He located the door. It was not locked, but the latch was stiff and he had to work hard to get it open. He was desperately afraid of making a noise and waking one of the family asleep upstairs.

Finally he was able to push the latch up. He opened the door just enough to slip inside. Immediately, he collided with a sharp-sided wooden chest. He paused for a moment, forbearing to swear and rubbing his leg. He knew this place was full of junk: crates of old bottles and china, oil lamps no longer in use, wine racks, broken chairs waiting to be mended. Very slowly, he groped his way forward – both arms extended in front of him – to where he guessed the stone staircase was that led up to the kitchen. He prayed that the door at the top was unlocked.

There were so many objects, large and small, to be negotiated there in the dark, to be felt around and avoided. It was crucially important to make no noise. Suddenly, his foot struck what seemed to be a pile of books, which toppled over, and he froze, waiting tensely for some minutes, listening for any sound of wakeful footsteps overhead. When he was sure there were none, he edged forward again. At last, he reached the place where he judged the stairs to be. He put out his hand to grip the banister rail. But it was not a rail that his hand encountered. It was the buttoned jacket of a figure standing there, absolutely still, at the foot of the stairs.

Paolo's mother, Rosemary Crivelli, lay rigid, flat on her back in her enormous bed, staring into the darkness. She had lain like this for hours, ever since she had retired to her room as usual and heard her son, Paolo, scrambling out of the pantry window to set off on his nightly sortie into Florence. Then came the seemingly endless wait for his return. It was impossible to sleep. She was too anxious. Her mind revolved around and around in its restless groove, reviewing the situation, wondering for the hundredth time whether she should confront him in the morning to finally let him know that she knew all about his adventures. She knew she should remind him of the dangers of what he was doing and forbid him – *forbid* him – to go out alone again at night, but somehow she could never find the heart to do it.

She knew it was her duty as a parent. He was her only son. But she knew too what her son's life was like, there at home in this joyless time, a thirteen-year-old boy with only his mother and sister and elderly Maria for company, his father far away for heaven knew how long. School was closed, there were no entertainments, there was a nightly curfew and the German military were a heavy presence in the city. She reflected grimly on the old cliché that wartime, when not terrifying, was a combination of long stretches of boredom and grinding hardship. It seemed that the Crivelli family were certainly getting their fair share of both. She knew very well how a boy like Paolo needed action, adventure, and a secret challenge that he thought nobody else knew about.

She had so many other anxieties to keep her awake too. In the darkness, she visualized a whole perspective of them, headed as always by the immediate challenge of how to get enough food for the family to eat tomorrow, of whether Maria's daily foray into the meagrely stocked market in Florence might yield something, and of whether the weekly bread ration would last out. Lurking beyond this were her thoughts of her daughter, Constanza, who was becoming increasingly uncommunicative. She seemed to want to do nothing all day but idly rearrange her hair in front of her mirror and pore over the old pre-war copies of French and American *Vogue* which lay about the house. Worse, there was her friendship with the Albertini family, who were among their few wealthy neighbours to have remained in Florence. Their daughter, Hilaria, was a year older than Constanza. The Albertinis had always been enthusiastic admirers of Italy's strutting dictator, Mussolini, who had allied their country with Nazi Germany and led them into this disastrous war.

Rosemary knew that Constanza's growing intimacy with openly Fascist sympathizers would hurt and anger her father if he knew about it. But she dared not interfere. Her position here in Florence was not an easy one. She was British by birth, Italian only by marriage. Now the British forces and their American allies had invaded Italy, landing in the south, and, after a long and bitter fight, were successfully pushing the German and Italian armies back. They already occupied Rome. It was only a matter of time before the fighting reached Florence.

She knew it was not safe for her or her children to show any particular political allegiance. Her husband, Franco Crivelli, had never made any secret of his opposition to Mussolini's government, its alliance with Nazi Germany and all that the Fascists stood for. It was because he was high on their wanted list that he had been forced to leave the family home and simply disappear. Not even Rosemary knew exactly where he was. It was better for her and her children that she did not.

She guessed he was working with the Partisans, those bands of recklessly brave anti-Fascist men and women who operated clandestinely in the hills around the city. Constantly on the move, they were secretly aided by local people. They engaged in all kinds of dangerous and subversive activities: blowing up bridges and railway lines to hamper German troop movements, ambushing transport trucks and helping Allied prisoners of war to escape and rejoin their units. They were known for their daring and their ruthlessness – and if they, or anyone associated with them, were caught, then death at the hands of the Gestapo was a gruesome certainty.

Rosemary had not been in contact with Franco

for months. It was too risky. To survive she had to maintain a low profile while trying to keep Paolo and Constanza out of trouble and praying for the day when they would be liberated by the Allies. She relied on the respect that was felt for her locally. She was well liked for the work she did with the Red Cross and charities associated with the Catholic Church. The priest and most local people were tactful enough not to press her on Franco's absence. But she was not above suspicion. She knew she was being watched. And recently she had sensed a certain reserve among her better-off neighbours like the Albertinis, even though she had always forced herself to be polite to them, however much she despised their politics.

Her own widowed mother was far away in bomb-blitzed London. Letters were the only means of communication, and they arrived very rarely. Rosemary wrote regularly with cheerful, carefully edited chit-chat, but she was not sure how many of those letters got through. Since Franco had left, she'd felt increasingly isolated and vulnerable.

She prayed a lot. Right now it was a prayer of gratitude that Paolo was safely back after another of his mad nocturnal excursions. He was growing up to be more and more like his intrepid father: a father whom, worryingly, he was now learning to live without. Small children, she reflected ruefully, could be protected to some extent, even in these desperate times. But teenagers were another matter entirely.

Now, quite apart from having to evade the attentions of the Gestapo, she was aware that the Partisans had marked her as a possible ally, and they were as ruthless as the German secret police. Despite her sympathy for the Partisan cause, she feared they might represent the worst danger yet by trying to involve her and her family in their plans. It had happened before. And tonight they would be out there in the dark, stealthy and determined, with guns slung over their shoulders – guns that were not intended for shooting rabbits.

In her room at the front of the house, Constanza was also lying awake, too anxious to sleep. Missing her father – "Babbo", as she and Paolo called him – was like a permanent ache in her life. And knowing how much Mamma must miss him too meant that she was always trying to keep her own feelings under control. As usual, she was trying to blot out the present by turning her mind to trivialities. Such as wondering, for instance, how long her lovely Ferragamo shoes – the ones which Babbo had given her before he had gone away – were going to last before they started to look shabby. And if, in the absence of even the remotest possibility of acquiring a new summer dress, she could persuade Maria to make her one from that fine white linen sheet she had found in the linen cupboard. But then, she thought fretfully, it would never be as smart as the kind of thing Hilaria wore every day and it would certainly not make her look like their favourite film star, Rita Hayworth. It was just awful being sixteen – very nearly seventeen – and never having anything nice to wear or being able to go to parties and dances as she imagined girls were doing in parts of the world far away from this relentless dreary war.

Constanza knew very well that if you had enough money you could buy smart clothes and shoes on the black market. The Albertinis had plenty of contacts there. But in her family that kind of behaviour would be thought totally immoral. Both her parents felt strongly that they must all share the pain of the shortages and lack of luxuries of any kind that was being endured by the ordinary hard-pressed Italian population. But sometimes, stuck up here in her room, Constanza wished that she wasn't expected to live up to such high standards. She seemed to be the only one who suffered. Her mother managed to look beautiful in everything she wore, however shabby, and Paolo was happy to wear any old clothes so long as he had his beloved bicycle.

At that moment she was roughly jolted from her thoughts by the sounds of Paolo arriving back from his nocturnal adventure. She suppressed a rising irritation with him for assuming that they were oblivious to what he was up to. So he needed the excitement – she didn't blame him for that – but if he only knew how tired and on edge he made them – especially Mamma, who was already so worried.

Constanza buried her head in her pillow and tried to empty her mind. All she wanted was a bit of peace, but this, it seemed, was impossible – and ten minutes later she was still wide awake.

Rosemary was also still lying tensely awake. She had winced when she'd heard Paolo on the shed roof and the pantry window slamming shut. *Poor Paolo!* she thought. How cross and humiliated he would be if he knew that every night she was lying awake and listening out for him. Now what? If only he would get on with it and come up to bed so that they could all get some badly needed sleep before dawn. She strained her ears, listening hard. After what seemed like a long time she heard him scrabbling about in the cellar, stumbling over things. What was he doing? She waited to hear his footsteps on the stairs but none came. Now, suddenly, there was dead silence.

Down in the cellar Paolo was standing frozen with fright. He expected a blow, or two hands reaching out from the darkness to lock in a stranglehold on his throat. But the figure a few feet away remained quite still. All he could hear was his own breathing. Agonizing minutes passed.

"Hello?" he whispered hoarsely. No answer. *"Hello?"*

Very cautiously, he reached out his hand and gently prodded the front of the buttoned jacket. There was no response. He felt his way slowly up towards the collar to where the face ought to be. There was no face, only a smooth wooden knob.

Paolo let out a great weary sigh of relief. It was

the old tailor's dummy that had stood in the cellar for years, displaying his dead grandfather's military dress uniform. Once it had been the object of great family pride. He remembered how the rows of gold buttons, the medals and the gold braid on the collar and cuffs had impressed him. Now he felt nothing but fury towards it for making such a fool of him, and he cursed it long and hard under his breath.

Then, legs leaden with exhaustion, he trudged up the stairs and tried the cellar door. It opened. Maria must have forgotten to lock it: his one piece of good fortune in an ill-fated night, he thought gloomily as he crept up to bed.

Rosemary heard him come up. She turned over, pulled the covers over her head and tried to sleep. But it was no good. Her limbs, carefully arranged in a sleeping position, failed to relax. Finally she gave up, stretched out again and lay there, watching the beginning of dawn already showing through the shutters.

CHAPTER 3

Maria knocked at Paolo's bedroom door and then bustled in without waiting for a reply. "Wake up, Paolo! It's late. Mass in half an hour!" Paolo buried his face in his pillow and pulled the bedclothes over his head. He longed to be left alone to drift back into sleep.

There had been a time, when he was a little boy, that Maria had been one of his favourite people. He had loved it when she came into his room, after he had gone to bed, bringing some choice titbits from the dinner that the grown-ups were having downstairs. He always tried to persuade her to sit on his bed and tell him fairy tales. But now her conversation bored him. It was mostly stale local gossip of the most banal kind, often repeated more than once.

She began tugging at his sheet. "Your mother and Constanza have had their breakfast and are already dressed for church. There's a clean shirt hanging in your cupboard. Come along now – up you get!"

Paolo groaned with irritation. Sundays were awful. He hated going to Mass. He wanted more sleep. But Maria was a force impossible to withstand. Grudgingly he staggered into the bathroom and dabbed his face, very briefly, with water. It was cold, as usual. Hot water was a great luxury in wartime and was rationed to a four-inch-deep bath once a week.

His mother and Constanza were waiting in the hall when, ten minutes later, he lurched downstairs. As usual, they were fresh and immaculate in their summer dresses, and each carried a black lace shawl, with which they would cover their heads at Mass, over one arm. Constanza did not bother to address a word to him.

She's so cool all the time, thought Paolo. *How does she manage it?*

Inwardly, had he known it, Constanza was far

from cool. She was tired after Paolo's nocturnal sortie into Florence had kept her awake, but that was the least of her concerns at that moment. Since Babbo had disappeared they had all been making a huge effort to act out a charade of normality, stepping carefully around one another. She herself had become increasingly good at pretending not to mind the family's isolation, sitting up in her room, playing her records. Sunday Mass often reminded her that most of the girls she had known at school were quietly avoiding her these days or else had moved away. No one had ever asked her point-blank where her father was. But they all knew that her mother was English and therefore one of the enemy – even though she had been an exemplary Italian wife and mother and had lived hospitably among them for so many years.

Hilaria Albertini was the only one among her friends who still wanted to see her. Although their families were so opposed politically it was good to have someone her own age drop in for a chat from time to time and swap fashion magazines. Constanza knew very well that the fluffy blonde hair, wide brown eyes and ready laugh concealed a core of tough self-interest, but Hilaria could be very good company and always knew all the latest gossip. Hilaria made Constanza feel the loss of her other friends less deeply. Moreover, Constanza knew it was important to keep up at least a superficially good relationship with the few neighbours left still willing to befriend the family. Constanza was only too aware of the precarious circumstances under which they were living – something that Paolo seemed to blithely disregard.

The Crivellis' house was a spacious villa with a sweep of gravel driveway, shuttered windows under wide overhanging eaves and a large terrace which ran the whole length of the house, overlooking the garden. In the days before the war there had been tennis parties, cocktails on the terrace and elaborate dinners with course after course that both Constanza and Paolo had seen being prepared in the kitchen by the cook and other servants. There had been joints of veal and game shot by their father, rich sauces, profusions of vegetables and wonderful puddings like the one – they had already forgotten the name of it – with hot, crisp meringue on the outside and ice cream spilling out from within. It made them ache with hunger just to think of it.

Paolo had been too young then to join the grown-ups and even Constanza had had to content herself with being presented in the drawing room for a brief time before dinner, her hair carefully parted on one side and held in place with those hair slides she hated. They were teenagers now and so old enough to attend, only there were no more parties, the garden was neglected and hardly anyone came to visit them, except Hilaria and the occasional priest.

The little church where they attended Mass was very near to their house. Set among cypress trees, it had once been a private chapel and part of the Crivelli estate. Now it was used as the local church for people from the village and surrounding farms. The bell was already tolling when they joined the usual sparse group gathered outside. They were mostly local farmers and their families, Maria's brother and his wife among them, and, of course, the Albertinis, who were out in force: Hilaria, her parents and her older brother, Aldo, all dressed up to the nines as usual. There were also three German Army officers, who were part of the occupying army stationed in Florence. They were Catholics and had been exempted from Sunday morning parade at their local barracks to attend Mass. They were very smart in their uniforms, with their belts and highly polished revolver holsters. There was the tall thin one who stood awkwardly on long, stork-like legs, and another, older man, already running to fat, who sported a small toothbrush moustache in imitation of his beloved leader, Adolf Hitler. The third and youngest was Lieutenant Helmut Gräss. He spoke good Italian and was exchanging polite conversation with Hilaria and Signora Albertini. He carried himself with a stiff, upright bearing that was at odds with his boyish face. He greeted Constanza and Rosemary eagerly with a heel-clicking salute.

Paolo stood apart with Maria, attempting a blank detached expression. He was well aware that, after Mass was over, worse was to follow: pre-lunch drinks with the Albertinis. Why did his mother go on accepting their invitations? he wondered. He knew she did not like them and hated to see Constanza being so friendly with Hilaria. The German officers were sure to be there too, not to mention Hilaria's smarmy brother, Aldo. He lived at home and had somehow been exempted from military service by wangling a well-paid job to do with supplying food to the German occupying forces. *And he is convinced that every woman in sight is in love with him,* thought Paolo. He closed his eyes wearily to avoid the sight of Aldo's jaunty, parrot-like profile engaged in what he thought was sparkling conversation. It was a relief when the bell stopped tolling and they all filed in to Mass.

The one good thing about drinks parties at the Albertinis' was the snacks. Nobody liked to ask where they got them because everyone knew they were only available on the black market, but that did not stop anyone from tucking in. Paolo had skilfully managed to manoeuvre himself into a corner to avoid the general conversation and still be near to a large plate of canapés. The guests were assembled on the terrace overlooking an impeccable sloping lawn. White-jacketed servants moved among them offering cocktails. Signor Albertini, as usual, had placed himself centre stage, overlooking his domain. Barrel-chested, he was immaculately suited, and wore a permanent smile, one which sometimes bordered on a grimace and which displayed a magnificent set of gold fillings. All the Albertinis, Paolo reflected, seemed to be equipped with more than the normal number of teeth, all of which were maintained by expensive dentistry. Indeed, the dentist himself was one of the guests, a pale, morose man, the sight of whom made Paolo wince. None of the local tenant farmers or their families were guests at the Albertinis'; they were not considered to be part of the upper-class Florentine circle. Only the big vineyard owners and wholesale vegetable growers – all of whom seemed to be doing very well in wartime – and professional people were invited.

The three German officers who had attended Mass were now joined by some others from their regiment. Most of them were gathered around either Hilaria or Constanza, laughing and chatting in a mixture of German and bad Italian. Hilaria was, as always, extra vivacious in the male company, giggling a lot and shaking back her blonde hair as she tried to keep them all amused. Paolo noticed how her eyes kept straying to Helmut, while his kept straying to Constanza. *It is as though everyone here is trying to pretend that the war is a million miles away instead of coming closer*

41

all the time, Paolo thought. He'd heard the reports about how the Allied armies were north of Rome and advancing towards Florence. There were rumours that the South African infantry brigades had already reached Orvieto and that the Indian division, which were fighting alongside the Allies, were attacking the German defence line north of Lake Trasimeno.

Constanza also knew of the Allies' progress but was careful not to bring it up in her conversation with the officers. In turn, they gave no hint as to the private state of their morale. Everyone knew that all leave had been cancelled and they were now on permanent alert, ready at all times to go into action.

As Lieutenant Gräss extricated himself from a conversation with Hilaria and made his way towards her, Constanza glanced over at her mother. She knew very well how much Rosemary disliked her being on friendly terms with the German officers. But it was necessary not to be seen to avoid them and, anyway, she liked Helmut Gräss. He spoke Italian well, treated her as one of the grown-ups and was prepared to have a proper conversation rather than merely engage in the lightly flirtatious social banter that his fellow officers were always rather unsuccessfully attempting.

Rosemary was standing to one side, chatting with Captain Roberto Spinetti, chief of the local *carabinieri*, the Florence military police force. They were old acquaintances. The captain had never approved of Franco Crivelli's anti-Fascist activities but he had always maintained a certain respect for him. And now Franco was gone, leaving the family socially isolated, the captain was trying to protect them in the German-occupied city, most particularly from the Gestapo. He bitterly resented their heavy-handed domination of the Italian civil police, undermining and sometimes countermanding his authority, even in his own office.

At that moment he and Rosemary were making small talk about food shortages.

"We still have supply lines coming in from the north," Captain Spinetti was saying, "but it's becoming increasingly difficult for me to give them a police escort. Two lorries of food were hijacked only last week … by black marketers or perhaps the Partisans. But my men are too overstretched here in Florence to catch them."

"We're managing to feed ourselves, just about," said Rosemary. "Although it is getting harder and harder. Especially with a boy Paolo's age. Teenage boys seem to have insatiable appetites."

"He's not yet of military age, is he?"

"No, only thirteen – he's tall for his age. I think he would welcome action of some kind. He gets so bored now school is closed for the vacation, and he so much misses…" She stopped short. She was about to say "his father" but quickly changed it to "the company of friends and young people of his own age, you know."

Just then there was a distinct lowering of the social temperature as a latecomer to the party, a sallow man in a civilian suit, was shown through the French windows onto the terrace.

Here he is, right on cue, like the demon in the pantomime, thought Paolo. It was Colonel Richter, the Gestapo secret police chief stationed in Florence. Captain Spinetti's conversation petered out in mid-sentence and his face froze. Signora Albertini went to greet the colonel effusively and began introducing him to some of her friends. Aldo, like a dog who scents someone unwrapping a tasty morsel, swiftly detached himself from a conversation at the other end of the terrace and oozed forward, all smiles, to shake the colonel by the hand. Power attracted him like a magnet.

The colonel was not particularly impressive physically. He was a nondescript man in his mid thirties who had made no attempt to cultivate a mustachioed military image. But his power could be felt in the way his pale eyes roamed sharply over the assembled guests, noting who was present, while seeming to converse politely with the Albertinis.

Rosemary quickly put down her glass. She caught Constanza's eye and signalled to her that it was time to leave. Paolo did not need to be told. He bid a silent and reluctant goodbye to the plate of canapés, even managing to slip a few into his pocket before joining his mother to make their polite farewells. As they exited onto the Albertinis' front drive they were joined by Lieutenant Gräss, who seemed to materialize out of nowhere.

"You are walking home? It would give me great pleasure to accompany you, but unfortunately, I have to report back to the barracks immediately. May I at least accompany you to the corner?"

"You're very kind," said Rosemary, "but no, really, we mustn't think of delaying you."

He paused, irresolute for a moment. Then he saluted smartly to Rosemary and gave what Paolo noticed was a special bow to Constanza before walking briskly away towards his car.

"I wish you wouldn't be quite so friendly with the German officers," Rosemary said as they made their way home. "You know how much Babbo would hate it."

"He was only being polite. And I thought we were rather rude, as a matter of fact," said Constanza coolly.

"He certainly seems to like clicking his heels at you," Paolo said, "but I suppose he's an improvement on Aldo, the Chinless Wonderboy. Talk about a stuffed parrot! I'd like to pour a whole jug of mayonnaise all over his head!"

Constanza did not bother to answer. She merely pulled her shawl over her brown arms. They all walked on in silence.

CHAPTER 4

When they arrived home Paolo hung about in the hall hoping to catch his mother alone. Last night's message was weighing heavily on him. Tight knots of anxiety filled his stomach every time he remembered those two armed men. But, after throwing down her things, Rosemary went straight into the kitchen to help Maria serve their meagre family lunch and when they had cleared away she went up to her room to rest.

All afternoon Paolo mooched around in the hot, parched garden, fretting about how he was going to pass on that message without giving away anything about his nocturnal sorties into Florence. He prided himself on being quite a good liar when the occasion demanded it, but somehow it was always particularly difficult when his mother was involved. She had a way of seeing through him.

From an open upstairs window, he could hear Constanza playing records on her wind-up portable gramophone. She seemed to be addicted to hearing the same tunes over and over again: Rina Ketty's French voice singing "J'attendrai", Edith Piaf's version of "La Vie en Rose", also in French, and, to annoy her mother, the German hit song "Lili Marlene".

Paolo wandered into the yard to see his dear old friend Guido. He felt that he was neglecting him these days but knew that Guido was too good-natured to hold it against him. The old dog lumbered out of his kennel with his usual rapturous welcome, putting his paws on Paolo's knees and trying to lick his face. Paolo fondled his ears and released his chain. It was too hot to go for a long walk, so together they ambled down to the olive grove at the end of the garden. Here, Guido ran ahead joyfully, rather wonky on one back leg but happy to be out and about and sniffing around everywhere. *If only life were always this simple,* thought Paolo, as he walked along behind, throwing a stick now and again.

It was nearly five o'clock when he returned Guido to his kennel and replenished his water supply from the tap in the yard. He would have liked to have given him something to eat, but, like the rest of the family, Guido was on strict food rationing and limited to the one daily meal of scraps which either Paolo or Maria fed him each morning.

Paolo hovered about on the terrace until Rosemary emerged and began watering the geraniums which rioted in huge terracotta pots along the low wall. He helped her carry the heavy old watering cans to and from the water tank. They worked together in silence for a while. Then he said casually, "Oh, by the way – I forgot to tell you, Mamma – I've got a message for you from two men I ran into on the road yesterday."

Rosemary stopped watering.

"Two men? What men? People we know?"

"Well, no, actually. I've never seen them before. It was when I was out on my bicycle."

"What did they want?"

"They wanted me to give you a message. They said to tell you they're in the area and they'll be getting in touch. Tonight, if they can. The usual way, they said."

"Was that all?"

"Yes, that was all. I only saw them for a few minutes."

Rosemary sat down rather suddenly on the terrace wall. There was a brief silence. To Paolo's surprise, she did not press him for any further details. She just sat there, her face dappled in deep shadow from the vine overhead. Then she got up and resumed her watering without another word.

That was easier than I expected, thought Paolo. But he felt uneasy. When his mother went indoors he wandered about the garden, unable to settle into doing anything. He felt useless and wished, not for the first time, that Babbo was there to take responsibility for everything. He resented him for being so utterly absent. It wasn't even as if he was a soldier serving away on the Russian front, or a prisoner of war. That would be something to brag about. And even prisoners managed to send letters or messages occasionally: to keep in touch somehow. Of course, Paolo and Constanza knew Franco had defied Mussolini and the German occupation and that he was probably out there in the hills somewhere with the Partisans and that he was some kind of hero. But you couldn't be

50

proud of someone *all* the time, especially when you couldn't talk about them to your friends. Nobody, not even Mamma, seemed to know where Babbo was but even if she did she wasn't going to tell Paolo and Constanza. It made Paolo long for some kind of a showdown, a huge row or a fight, anything to break down the wall of avoidance and silence. But he was not allowed even that. His mother's loneliness and vulnerability ruled out any angry confrontations.

He picked up a scythe and went to work off his pent-up feelings on the weeds and stinging nettles that grew in profusion all over what used to be the formal garden. *It is almost a relief,* he thought, *that the war, the real fighting, is getting ever closer.*

Rosemary did not attend Mass again that evening. Instead, she roamed the house, plumping up cushions, sorting laundry, finding things to tidy up while keeping an anxious eye on the garden. Paolo seemed to be staying out there until long after dark. She caught a glimpse of him now and again, prowling aimlessly about.

Supper that evening was leftovers from lunch and consisted only of rather stale bread, salad and a little cheese. Food rationing was too tight now to allow for more than one main family meal a day. Constanza appeared briefly and then retreated back to her room. Paolo came in late, ate very little and then he too went upstairs.

At nine o'clock Rosemary and Maria listened to the news on the old radio set in the kitchen. It was in Italian and so heavily censored by German-controlled broadcasting that it was very difficult to get any clear picture of what was actually happening. There was a lot of talk about "brave resistance to enemy advances" but nothing specific. The only source of information now was rumour, and that was mostly unreliable too.

At last, when the whole house was quiet, Rosemary went up to her room. She did not undress. Instead, she sat fully clothed by her window, looking out at the garden, waiting and listening. Just after midnight she opened her bedroom door very quietly and slipped out onto the landing. Paolo and Constanza's bedroom lights were out. She listened for a while at both their doors. There was no sound. She crept downstairs.

In spite of the hot night the shutters in the big drawing room which overlooked the garden were closed and the curtains tightly drawn. Total blackout was rigidly enforced, and there were heavy fines for any householder who showed a chink of light that might be spotted by enemy aircraft. She turned out all the lights, pulled back the curtains, undid the shutters and opened the French windows. She stepped out onto the terrace.

There was no moon. She hesitated for a moment, peering into the darkness, then descended the steps and crossed the expanse of rough dried-up grass that had once been a lawn. Beyond it was a gate that opened onto a narrow path, densely overshadowed by a row of cypress trees. The cicadas were keeping up their incessant sound; otherwise all she could hear were her own footsteps.

The path petered out into an unkempt grove of olive trees. They lurched at grotesque angles over a litter of casually dumped garden refuse and discarded wine barrels, half hidden in weeds. At the end was a long empty shed and in its shadow Rosemary saw the pinpoints of three lit cigarettes glowing in the dark.

CHAPTER 5

Three men stood there, huddled together, the outline of their rifles silhouetted against the sky. They all wore caps, pulled well down, making it impossible to see their faces.

As Rosemary approached, one of them threw down his cigarette and said quietly, *"Signora? Signora* Crivelli?"

"Yes." With a stab of fear she realized that the man beside him had now lowered his rifle and was pointing it at her.

"We need to speak with you, *signora.* You know who we are, I think?"

She knew who they were, all right. The Partisans. These men were probably led by Il Volpe – the Fox

– a local leader whom hardly anyone claimed to have encountered in person. A man who, Rosemary suspected, was trying to draw her and her son into helping them.

"What do you want with me?" Rosemary asked, trying to keep her voice steady.

"We don't intend you or any of your family harm, *signora*. We want your help, that's all. Just a little help, like the last time." He paused. The man with the rifle shifted uneasily.

"Things are different now," said Rosemary. "It's far more dangerous. The Gestapo are watching us all the time."

The first man ignored this and went on urgently, "It would only be for one night. We need to bring two men in close to the city, to put them into contact with friends who will help them."

"What men?"

"Who they are need not concern you too closely, *signora*. The less you know, the better."

"You mean Allied servicemen? Escaped prisoners of war who you are trying to get back to their own lines?"

This was greeted by silence, but Rosemary

knew she was right. She had been asked to do this before, several times, and on each occasion she had unwillingly co-operated while desperately wishing that she had never, ever become involved. She had done it for Franco's sake. But she knew very well what a terrifying risk she was taking. She thought of Paolo and Constanza and what would happen to them if she were arrested. They had both been away at school before and known nothing about it. But now…

"I can't—" she began.

But the man cut in. "Just one night – that's all we ask."

His voice was persuasive, but the rifle still pointing directly at her was more so. Rosemary was silent. These people were as ruthless as the enemy, especially now the Allies were so close. They were eagerly awaiting the time when they could rise up out of hiding and fight alongside them.

She tried to think about Franco and what he would want her to do. But instead, her mind was filled by thoughts of Paolo on his bicycle, riding at night through the empty streets, and what might happen to him – or any of them – if she did not co-operate.

"Very well," she said at last. "For one night only…"

"Good. It will be soon. We'll be in touch to let you know when."

Rosemary hurried back to the house with her arms huddled about her. She was shivering, not with cold but with fear. She was only just beginning to realize the full implications of what she had agreed to do. But she would have been far more terrified if she had known that as the three men melted away into the darkness, her son, Paolo, was following them.

Paolo had known all evening that there was a certain tension in the air. Although his mother's reaction to the message had been non-committal, he sensed that she had something on her mind, so he was keeping an eye on things. This, he told himself, was what detective work was all about. It was one of the skills he was planning on practising professionally one day when he was grown up.

When he got to his bedroom he settled down to wait until he heard Rosemary come upstairs. A long silence followed. He could sense her sitting there in her room, wide awake. At last, after what seemed like an endless time, he heard her re-emerge and creep out onto the landing, where she paused outside his door. He held his breath and prayed that she wouldn't look in. Then he heard her go downstairs. Cautiously, he poked his head out of his bedroom window, which overlooked the terrace, and saw her flit across the dark garden. Within minutes he was following her.

As he drew near to the shed he crouched low in the bushes. The sight of his mother in conversation with three armed men gave his stomach a lurch of fear mixed with excitement. He was pretty sure who they were. The Partisans. The men whom he had admired so much and for so long but had never met until last night. And now here they were, armed, in his own back garden. He couldn't imagine why they were here or what business they could possibly have with his mother. He strained his ears to hear but it was no good; they were speaking too softly. When Rosemary hurried back to the house, he watched the men set off into the darkness. He waited a few more minutes. Then, not thinking why he was doing it, he followed them, keeping well into the shadows of the trees that bordered the track.

After skirting the turning to the farm where

Maria's brother lived, the way continued sharply upwards, past the terraced vines that sprawled out across the hillside. The path became stonier, hardly a track at all, winding up into the dense scrub and olive trees that grew on the higher ground. Paolo was painfully aware of his every footfall. And he was terrified of what would happen if the men turned around and spotted him. But he knew these hills well. He had roamed around them since childhood and he had a good idea of where these men were heading. Somewhere up here the path ran alongside a deep gully with a dried-up river bed, very overgrown. It was an ideal place for a camp hideout.

He had kept the men in sight but then, quite suddenly, he lost them. Sweating with exhaustion, he paused and peered ahead. There was no sign of them. They had vanished.

Paolo stood quite still in the darkness. There was no sound except for the rustling of dry grass. Fear came down on him like a cold hand. Before, he had hardly thought about the risk he was running by following the men onto the lonely hillside in the middle of the night. Now he remembered those rifles, and the stories of the kind of treatment the Partisans handed out to spies. Despite his fear, a plan formed in his mind – but now was not the time to put it into action. He turned around and scrambled back the way he had come, expecting at every turn to meet an armed figure looming up at him out of the darkness, perhaps even a man with the eyes of a fox.

CHAPTER 6

It was after three o'clock in the morning when Paolo reached home. He was tired out. Rosemary had locked the house up again, so there was nothing for it but to stay out all night and appear just before breakfast, pretending he had been for an early morning stroll. He hoped his dishevelled state would not arouse suspicion. For what was left of the night, he huddled down on one of the garden seats on the veranda.

He was dozing there when, three short hours later, his mother came across him as she stepped out into the early morning sunshine. He was amazed at how normal she seemed considering the events of a few hours ago.

"Up early, Paolo?"

"Yes. I've been for a bike ride."

"Good. Now, I want you and Constanza to cycle into Florence this morning. There's a chance of some bread and pasta in the market today and maybe some vegetables and cheese. It's too much for Maria to carry. Hurry up and have your breakfast, then you can start right away before it gets too hot."

Paolo was drooping with exhaustion as he slowly assembled the shopping baskets and got out his bike. Constanza appeared reluctant to leave. She came out of the house slowly, wearing one of Babbo's old cotton shirts, her feet thrust into a pair of leather sandals.

"I suppose I've got to ride Maria's ancient bone-shaker," she said. The sun was already uncomfortably hot by the time they had pumped up the tyres. They were both silent as they freewheeled down the hill into the city.

As they drew closer to the outskirts it became obvious that many other people were on the same errand. Most were on foot, carrying baskets, and some were pushing handcarts.

There was an atmosphere of tension everywhere. German troops were a heavy presence, and many streets were sealed off. By the time Paolo and Constanza arrived at the market they found it already packed with a bad-tempered scrum. There was a great deal of pushing and shoving, good manners having long since evaporated in the grim struggle to get enough food to feed a family.

Constanza was surprisingly good at this sort of thing. She managed to elbow her way deftly to the front of the crowd, choosing only the market stallholders whom she knew were honest, and making no attempt to bargain with them. She just pointed firmly to the goods she wanted and waved the money, while Paolo struggled behind with the bicycles and filled up their baskets.

They were both sweating and dishevelled when they managed to extricate themselves from the crowd and so stopped to wash their hands and faces at a wall fountain. Paolo was so tired that he could hardly think straight. And there was still the prospect of the long, heavy-laden pull uphill to their home.

They were sitting dejectedly side by side on the stone rim of the fountain basin when Hilaria Albertini suddenly appeared, tripping up the street in high heels and a white linen dress, as fresh as if she had just stepped out of a beauty parlour. Her blonde hair was swept up elaborately above her forehead and curled in an immaculate long bob at the back.

"Constanza! *Carissima!* What ever are you doing here?" she said. Then, "Oh, hello, Paolo. Been shopping?"

Paolo didn't reply, but Constanza managed a confident smile.

"At the market," she said. "It was awful. What are you doing, Hilaria?"

"Oh, I got a lift in with Aldo in his car. He's gone off to some kind of high-level meeting somewhere. But all these people! I can't think why they all choose to come into the city when there's so much military traffic here already."

"They need food, I suppose," said Constanza. Her tone was neutral.

"Oh yes – of course. Aldo gets all our stuff delivered for us."

"Where from?" Paolo asked pointedly.

"Oh, I don't know. I leave all that sort of thing to him and Mamma. Though things are so difficult for her at the moment, poor darling, with hardly any servants."

"I love your shoes," said Constanza, changing the

subject. They were all regarding Hilaria's feet when a shadow fell across them. A large open German military car had drawn up with two uniformed officers in the back. One of them jumped out. It was Lieutenant Gräss. Hilaria quickly adjusted her legs into a demure fashion-model pose. The lieutenant saluted her politely, but it was Constanza he was looking at.

"You have been to the market, I see," he said, indicating their loaded bicycles. "I wish I could offer to help with your heavy burdens. But I have a great deal to do, things being as they are. You really should avoid coming into the city if you can, you know."

"We have to eat," said Constanza simply.

"What's the latest news, Helmut?" Hilaria asked, looking up at him, wide-eyed. "Is the fighting really getting closer? You know everything that's happening, of course. We poor civilians know nothing. Are we going to be shelled? Or bombed?"

Helmut inclined his head very slightly to indicate that of course he was not at liberty to answer.

"You must stay in your house and not go out unless it is absolutely necessary," was all he said, still addressing himself to Constanza and Paolo.

"It is not wise to go out into any of the countryside surrounding your home. There was a major incident to the north of the city quite recently. Four of our army personnel and two Italian drivers were killed."

"The Partisans, you mean?" said Paolo.

"Yes. They are armed and very dangerous. If you have any information of their whereabouts, or see anything suspicious, you must report it at once."

Hilaria shivered with exaggerated fear.

"But of course we will," she said eagerly.

"Now I must insist that you return to your homes as soon as you can." He glanced over his shoulder. His fellow officer made an impatient gesture. Helmut saluted again and jumped back into the car. Then the driver revved the engine and they were gone.

"Well, I must be on my way too," said Hilaria brightly. "Helmut is quite right, of course; we shouldn't stay here too long. I must run if I'm going to catch Aldo. So sorry we can't give you a lift home." She made as if to go, then turned round, smiling, and said, "What a pity you have to wear that old shirt, Constanza. Is it one of your father's cast-offs? And, by the way, where exactly *is* your father these days? We all long to know."

CHAPTER 7

After they had arrived home and unpacked the shopping baskets, Paolo had a short snooze and awoke refreshed. For the rest of the day he made himself useful, helping Maria to hang up the family washing she had toiled over all morning. Maria always did the laundry in the big stone sink, up to her elbows in soapsuds, and then wrung it out by hand. The two of them draped the sheets over some low bushes to bleach in the sun and pegged out the rest on the clothes-lines. When they had finished Paolo asked her if there was anything else he could do. Maria reacted with mild surprise. Then she put her arms around him.

"You're a good boy, Paolo," she said. "How could

your mamma and I manage without you? But run along now. I'll let you know if there's anything you can do to help me later."

Suddenly Paolo felt tears prick his eyes and turned away to hide them. He wished she hadn't said that, treating him like a kid, today of all days. He had been thinking of nothing but his plan since the night before. Absolutely no one must know about it, and especially not his mother or Maria. He was like someone standing at the top of a high diving board, waiting to jump. Their trip into Florence that morning and the realization of how close they were to being engulfed by the war had strengthened his resolve. Being scared only made him even more determined.

When Rosemary and Maria had retired for a siesta and Constanza had gone up to her room to play her interminable gramophone records, Paolo slipped quietly into the yard and eased his bicycle out of the shed. He was carrying his small rucksack, which he had packed with food and water and a few other things he judged necessary. It was the sight of Guido, rousing himself stiffly from his kennel to greet him with the old enthusiastic affection, which finally brought Paolo to tears. He brushed them away with his arm, knelt down and spoke to the old dog, fondling his ears and saying goodbye in a low voice, promising to take him for a walk soon. Then he was on his way, pedalling past the farm, which lay wrapped in mid-afternoon silence, and off up the track in the direction he had taken the night before.

It was not long before the going got too rough and steep to ride. He did not want a puncture. He was by no means sure that he would encounter the Partisans. He knew they were on the move all the time and were taking more care than ever to maintain their cover. Not even Maria's brother at the farm, who knew every inch of the surrounding countryside and all the local gossip, would know their exact whereabouts. That kind of knowledge was too dangerous to reveal. But somehow or other Paolo would find them, because he was determined to join them.

And why not? He knew that there were plenty of boys of sixteen who had done it, and he was tall for his age. He could use a rifle; his father had taught him. He wanted to fight, to be part of the action: no longer hanging about aimlessly at home. He knew that the coming months, weeks even, were crucial to the next phase of the war and he was determined to play a part in it.

He still didn't really understand why the Partisans had wanted to meet his mother. What part could *she* possibly play in their plans? Was it something to do with his father? Paolo hoped that by joining them he would be the better able to protect her.

He pressed on doggedly in the shimmering heat, following every turn in the track as he remembered it from the night before. But he was beginning to wonder if he had taken the right way after all. Things looked so different in daylight and there was no sign of the dried-up river bed. He paused to get his breath, regretting that he had brought his bicycle. It was useless up here anyway.

Suddenly, out of the corner of his eye, he saw three men. They were standing, very still, looking down at him from the top of the nearby bank. One of them lifted his rifle to his shoulder and pointed it straight at him. Paolo froze. There was a long pause. Then one of them said something in a low voice he couldn't catch, and the three came down the bank with leisurely menace and stood in his path.

"What are you doing here?" one asked. "Looking for someone, are you?"

"Yes, I was. I mean – I am looking for you, I think."

"You think?"

Paolo forced himself to keep his voice steady. "Yes. If you are … who I think you are … I would like to join you."

They looked at him in silence. These men had made no attempt to hide their faces. Their skin was tanned a deep brown, and they were slung about with ammunition belts and wore grubby red bandanas around their necks. They were Partisans all right, but Paolo had a feeling that they were not the ones he had encountered on the road the other night.

One of them cracked into a contemptuous grin.

Paolo trembled but he spoke up as confidently as he could. "I would like to join you," he repeated. "I know this area well and I can use a rifle. I can be useful in other ways too. I can take messages. No one will suspect me."

The grinning man said something to his comrade in a low voice. Then he took a step nearer and prodded Paolo in the chest with the end of his rifle.

"Walk," he said.

Paolo turned and walked, pushing his bicycle with one hand. Things were not going to plan. This was not the reception he had envisaged. Even though they moved in silence, he was painfully aware of the three men behind him. When he reached a fork in the track Paolo hesitated. Another prod of the rifle.

"Keep going."

But as Paolo moved forward again, he tripped. One of the men had stuck his foot out and hooked Paolo's leg, tripping him up. He sprawled to the ground and his bicycle crashed down beside him. Paolo lay there, furious, while the man who had tripped him up grabbed his bicycle and passed it to one of his comrades.

"On your feet," he told Paolo.

Paolo got up. He tried to keep his voice steady. "That's my bicycle. Give it back please."

They all guffawed. Then the man who had tripped him gestured to the track with his rifle.

"You can walk home from here, sonny," he said. "Get back to your mamma. This isn't a kid's war. You can try to find us next year if you like – except we won't be around."

"But my bicycle—"

"We'll be hanging on to that. We could use another bike."

"But it's mine!"

"Not any more, it isn't. And if you let on a word about what happened to it there'll be trouble for you and your family – *capito*? Understand?"

Perhaps it was sheer exhaustion that made him so foolhardy, but ignoring the rifle that was still pointing at him, he lunged at the man holding his bicycle. Seizing the handlebars, he tried to drag it off him. There was a brief tussle. Then the third man grabbed him by the shoulders, swung him round and punched him hard in the stomach. Paolo doubled up. The pain was excruciating. He was kicked from behind and found himself on the ground again.

He rolled into a ball, covering his head with his arms in anticipation of another blow. Then he heard a voice say, "*Basta!* Enough!"

Two hands reached down and yanked him back onto his feet. He stood there gasping.

A fourth man was holding him firmly by the scruff of his neck, something that Paolo welcomed because his legs seemed no longer able to support him. The man was stocky and powerfully built and dressed in the typical faded blue cotton trousers that local peasants wore for work; ammunition belts were strapped over his shoulders and around his waist. He wore very good leather boots laced up to the knee, and his cap was pulled down well over his eyes. The lower half of his face was covered by a moustache and several days' growth of tawny red beard. He was armed with a rifle, like the others, but it was slung across his back.

What now? thought Paolo groggily, steeling himself for the next assault.

To his relief, his three assailants lowered their weapons and stood back sullenly, one still stubbornly gripping Paolo's bicycle. This fourth man was clearly a figure of some authority.

"What's going on here?" he asked abruptly.

"Just a kid nosing around where he shouldn't. Thinks he can act tough. Wants to join us – but look at him!"

"Is that his bicycle?"

"Yeah. It could be useful to us."

The bearded man turned to Paolo. "What's your name?"

"Crivelli. I am Paolo Crivelli. I live…" He

hesitated as the man's grip tightened on his neck.

"Crivelli? You are *Signora* Crivelli's boy?"

"Yes. I'm thirteen and I can…"

But his interrogator had already turned back angrily to the others.

"*Stupidi! Ignoranti!* What d'you think you're playing at? I suppose you didn't think of asking his name before you started roughing him up? You could wreck everything and get us all shot!" Then he let go of Paolo, grabbed the bicycle and shoved it back at him. "Take it – go home – *presto!* – as soon as you can. And remember, you say nothing about this little adventure to your family – nothing – understood?" Then he turned to go and gestured to the others to follow him.

"But I want—" said Paolo weakly.

"Just get going – *now*!"

Paolo could resist no longer. Forlorn, dejected and utterly humiliated, he set off, bumping dangerously down the track on his bike and praying that the sharp stones wouldn't wreck his tyres.

CHAPTER 8

When Paolo pedalled wearily down the lane and into the yard he found Maria waiting anxiously, shading her eyes with her hand.

"Paolo!" she cried. "Wherever have you been? We've been looking all over for you. Your mamma wants you, right away."

This was the last thing that Paolo wanted to hear. All he wanted to do now was go to his room, lie on the bed with the shutters closed and try to come to terms with his utter humiliation. His plan to become a hero of the resistance – fighting alongside his fellow Partisans for his country's freedom – now seemed merely childish. That was what those men had thought anyway. He hated them for the way they'd treated him, but that only made him more determined to join them – to prove his worth and show them that he was as tough as they were.

He slouched into the hall, where he found Constanza sitting on the stairs. Unusually for her, she jumped up when she saw him and took his arm.

"Thank goodness you're back. Something's up, Paolo. Mamma's in a bit of a state – you know, all icy calm but pacing about a lot. I'm glad you're here. She wouldn't say anything to me until you got back."

They found Rosemary in the kitchen, assembling empty wine bottles in a very precise row on the big wooden table.

"You wanted to talk to us, Mamma?"

"Yes – come and sit down, both of you." They sat. She took a chair and faced them. They knew this was serious.

"My dears … my dearest dears…" She paused, gulped and tried again. "I know I can trust you both completely. This has to be only between us. Maria knows, but of course she would never say anything. I've promised, you see. And it's only for one night, so we'll just have to get through it as best we can."

"Get through what?" asked Constanza.

"Some people will be coming here tomorrow night. I got the message this afternoon. I don't know who they are. They'll be complete strangers. But I've agreed to let them stay here – to let them *hide* here – for one night only. Then they must be gone."

There was a brief pause while Constanza and Paolo digested this information in silence.

"Maria and I have been making preparations to accommodate them in the cellar," explained Rosemary. "Food and water, and somewhere for them to lie down and get some sleep if they can. And I want you two to carry on absolutely normally. In fact, it would be better if you don't see or talk to them at all. I will be going to tomorrow's evening Mass as usual and I want you to have supper and go to bed early. If you hear any unexpected sounds in the night take no notice and, whatever happens, don't come downstairs. Is that understood?"

Paolo was still too amazed to answer. But Constanza said coolly, "It's the Partisans, isn't it? They're bringing escaped prisoners of war here, helping them to get back to their units and fight again on the Allied side."

Rosemary did not react to this immediately. She clasped her hands together very tightly.

"How did you know this?" she asked at last.

"Oh, Mamma – we're not kids any more. Of course we can guess what's happening and we know why you're helping them: it's what Babbo would expect from us."

"Yes … yes. Do you think I would do otherwise? But Constanza – *carissima* – you must try to understand why I can't involve you. That, too, is what your father would expect from me. I know it's hard. It may even seem exciting to you. But it's not a game – it's too serious. You know what will happen if we're found out."

She turned to Paolo beseechingly, half expecting him to say something. But he was still too surprised to speak. It was all coming together: the message he had carried, that conversation between his mother and those men behind the shed. Why hadn't he guessed before? While he was pursuing his wild goose chase up in the hills, trying to join the Partisans, the real action had been going on right here in his own home. "Don't worry, Mamma. You can rely on us," he said bravely.

CHAPTER 9

The next morning the Crivelli family stayed close to the house and tried to maintain a normal routine. Neither Paolo nor Constanza went near the cellar, though they knew that by now everything had been made ready for – for whom, exactly? They both wondered, but knew better than to ask.

The house was unnaturally calm and silent. Then, at about noon, a motorcycle roared up the drive and the front doorbell rang. Rosemary, who was carrying a couple of blankets and a loaf of bread across the hall to the cellar, froze. Hardly anyone came to their front door these days. Maria laboured slowly out of the kitchen to answer it. Rosemary only just had time to kick the cellar door closed before Lieutenant

Helmut Gräss entered the hall, followed by Maria. He was in battledress, wearing his service revolver and steel helmet.

He saluted smartly and said, "Forgive this intrusion, *Signora* Crivelli. We are checking the whole area to see that all civilians are at home. There is a great deal of troop movement on the roads, which cannot be impeded."

He paused as his gaze fell on the blankets and bread that Rosemary was clutching. But before he could say anything else, Constanza appeared behind her mother. She had heard the conversation from upstairs and had come down to give her mother some moral support. *I've got to get Helmut outside somehow,* she thought anxiously. *Mamma's not a good liar.*

"You must have so much to do," she said to the lieutenant. "But can't we offer you something to eat or drink?"

"A glass of water only, please, if you would be so kind."

As Maria hurried away to fetch it, Constanza manoeuvred Gräss gently outside. It was shimmeringly hot. The sky was a fathomless Italian blue and the shadows of the cypress trees that sheltered the house from the road laid cool, dark fingers on the gravel. It was hard to believe that not far away young men around Helmut's age were hell-bent on killing one another. The German officer and Constanza stood beside his motorcycle and he took off his helmet. Without it, he looked years younger.

"We will be in action soon," he said. "I hoped I would see you today because I wanted to say ... I wanted to tell you..."

Maria appeared with his glass of water and he stopped speaking to gulp it down. When she had gone indoors he began again.

"There's so much to say, if it were possible. But so little time. You are half English, of course. And your father..."

"My father is away from home, as you know. We none of us know his whereabouts at the moment."

"My father is in a difficult position too," said Helmut quietly. "We are a military family. He is a colonel, a professional soldier. He served in the last war and now, more recently, with General Rommel in North Africa, but he has never been in agreement with the Nazi high command and what they are

82

doing to our country. It has put him, and his career, into considerable danger. I want you to know this. I can tell you because I trust you, and your family. I cannot bear that we should be enemies, because I … you are…" And then, without realizing it, he lapsed into German, speaking so softly and urgently that Constanza, who understood the language only slightly, could hardly follow what he said. Though she thought she caught the words "so dear to me".

Eventually he fell silent and took her hand. He was looking at her so intently that she hardly knew how to reply. Then, abruptly, he straightened himself, handed her back the empty glass and put on his helmet. Without another word, he kicked the engine of his motorcycle into life and drove off down the drive.

Constanza stood there for a moment looking after him. She really liked Helmut. He was the kind of young man, she reflected, that her father would have got on well with, had they met in some other, happier world: one in which they were not fighting on bitterly opposed sides. She realized what a compliment he had paid her by telling her about his own father and background. He was such a serious man, made more serious still by the enormous weight of responsibility which had been put upon him as a German officer at war. He was not many years older than she was – twenty or twenty-one, perhaps – and it touched her that he had not been able to express his feelings for her except in his own beloved language. It was difficult for her to think of him as The Enemy, someone against whom she and her family were about to pit all their courage and ingenuity. Slowly, she turned around and wandered thoughtfully back into the house.

CHAPTER 10

That evening neither Paolo nor Constanza made any fuss about taking themselves off to their rooms very early. But not, of course, to sleep. The tension in the house meant that was out of the question. As darkness fell, Maria too retired to her own quarters off the kitchen, leaving Rosemary alone to pace nervously from room to room. She turned off all the downstairs lights, keeping only one burning in the hall, then opened the windows of the drawing room, which gave onto the terrace.

It was a still, hot night, full of stars. Somewhere out on the main road she could hear heavy vehicles – German tanks and military trucks, probably – rumbling towards the city. Then all was silent. She lit a cigarette, smoked half of it in a vain attempt to calm herself and then stabbed the rest out in disgust. She went once more to the window. Out there beyond the terrace, where the trees cast dense shadows on the parched grass, she thought she caught a glimpse of a slight movement. A man detached himself from the dappled gloom of the hedge and came stealthily towards the house.

Summoning all her courage, she went outside and paused at the top of the steps, peering into the dark.

"Buona sera," she said stiffly.

"Buona sera, signora."

She could see his rifle but not his face, which was hidden under the peak of his cap.

"You'd better come in."

The man turned back a few paces and gave a low whistle. At the sound, two other figures emerged from the darkness. She beckoned, and all three men filed inside.

Rosemary shuttered and closed the French windows, drew the curtains and switched on the lights, then turned to face them. All three were dressed more or less alike in Italian work clothes, but the two younger men were unarmed. One was tall, broad-shouldered and dark. The other man was slighter and very fair with a small moustache. Both looked thin and unkempt and had dark circles of fatigue under their eyes.

The older man was sweating heavily. He removed his cap and loosened his scarf to reveal close-cropped hair, small slightly slanting eyes and several weeks' growth of rusty red beard. Rosemary turned towards his two younger companions, who, she realized, were not much older than her own daughter.

"You must be tired," she said. "You'll be sleeping in the cellar here – not very comfortable, I'm afraid, but we've made up some mattresses on the floor and it's quite dry. But first, you must be hungry. We've prepared something for you to eat, if you'd care to follow me…"

They looked at her blankly and shuffled their feet.

"They don't understand, *signora*," explained their companion. "They don't speak any Italian."

"Oh – of course. Forgive me."

After she had repeated herself in English, both young faces visibly relaxed. The tall dark one gave her a grin of gratitude. "Thanks, ma'am. It's real kind of you, what you're doing for us. And yes, we sure would appreciate something to eat."

He's American, or possibly Canadian, thought Rosemary. She smiled at him and turned to his companion.

"It's most awfully good of you," said the fair one. He had the kind of unmistakable English voice that Rosemary had not heard for a long time. It made her heart contract with a sudden pang of homesickness for the country she had left so many years ago, a country which, for all she knew, no long existed as she remembered it. She wanted to ask him where he came from and about his family and how he had been taken prisoner. But she knew that this was not the moment for conversation. And, anyway, the less she knew about these uninvited guests, the better. Instead, she picked up a small oil lamp and said simply, "Follow me."

The makeshift accommodation that she and Maria had prepared in the cellar was indeed very primitive but it was as welcoming as they could make it. Some plates of food, a pitcher of water and a bottle of wine were laid out on an upturned packing case and the two young men fell on it ravenously. They ate in silence, then slumped down on the mattresses, heads and shoulders drooping with fatigue, already nearly asleep.

Rosemary turned to address the older man, but he had already disappeared. She found him in the hall, preparing to leave.

"One night only, remember," she warned him, keeping her voice as steady as she could.

"Yes, yes, *certo*. But I have to tell you we may need your help in another small way, *signora*."

"That's out of the question. I'm already putting myself and my family in a dangerous situation, as you well know. You mustn't ask any more of us…"

"It's essential to our plan, I'm afraid. I wouldn't ask it of you otherwise, and besides it's already arranged. Tomorrow night we have to get these two men into Florence, where some of our people – never mind who – will be waiting to take them out of the city. They will then be able to rejoin their units in time for the next big push northwards. It will not be long now before Florence is in Allied hands."

"I know all this. But I insist that you remember my position."

"Of course. But these two men can't speak Italian.

If they go unaccompanied into the city and are stopped by the police or a German military patrol – which is more than likely – they'll certainly need someone with them, someone above suspicion … a member of your household, perhaps?"

There was a long pause as this sank in. Rosemary was too shocked even to feel fear. She burst out angrily, "How can you suggest that? Do you think I would allow anyone – anyone at all – to risk such a venture? No one, not even you, has a right to ask such a thing of us."

The man made no reply. He was not looking at her but over her shoulder at the staircase. She glanced round. Halfway up the first flight of stairs, in the dark, sat a figure watching them through the banister rails.

"Paolo!" gasped Rosemary. "How long have you been there?"

He got to his feet, embarrassed. When at last he spoke it was not to his mother. Instead, he addressed himself directly to the man he now recognized as the one who had given him the message for his mother – the same man he had encountered up in the hills, the one who had rescued him and then restored his bicycle to him when he had thought it lost for good.

Now he was almost sure he knew who this man was – Il Volpe himself.

"I could go," he said. "I'll take my bicycle. No one will suspect me. I'm a local boy. They know me. I could do it."

CHAPTER 11

The next morning, while their two clandestine guests slept the sleep of total exhaustion in the cellar, the rest of the Crivelli household was in turmoil. Maria was in no shape to be of any use at all. She was convinced that the Gestapo would come at any second and they would all be shot. Rosemary herself was distraught. She felt she was being sucked into an escalating nightmare of danger, involving not only herself but now her family. She had never, ever, fought with Paolo about anything as big as this before. Arguments and family rows, yes; but this brick wall of blatant disobedience and indifference to her entreaties was new to her. Last night this mad scheme involving Paolo as an escort for two escaping Allied prisoners of war had been simply foisted on her. It had all been arranged before Il Volpe had disappeared off into the darkness, and this morning all Paolo would say was: "It'll be all right, Mamma. It'll only take an hour or two and then I'll be back, I promise."

Constanza was anxious too. *He seems to think he's the hero in some kind of adventure movie,* she thought as she watched her brother nonchalantly eating his breakfast. *Does he really have no idea how dangerous this is?* Harbouring two escaped prisoners of war in the cellar was crazily risky. But the whole enterprise had gone much too far now for either her or her mother to do anything about it.

Things only got worse as the day wore on. It became obvious that it was useless for either Constanza or Paolo to avoid all contact with their guests in the cellar. When the two men woke at about noon, Paolo kept guard in the deserted yard and tried to stop Guido from barking while they slipped out to wash themselves under the cold tap. Maria was refusing point-blank to have anything to do with them, so it was Constanza who took them their food.

The two young men, sitting crouched on their mattresses in the semi-dark, were bored as well as scared, and desperate for company. Even in that dim light, the sight of Constanza did a lot to improve their morale and they tried hard to detain her as they ate.

Constanza's English was good. Now she wished it were better. But she was able to discover that the young fair-haired Englishman was Flight Lieutenant David Graham, an RAF pilot whose Spitfire had been shot down near Monte Cassino. After bailing out with only minor injuries, he had been treated in a German military hospital and then transferred to a prisoner-of-war camp near Bologna. His companion was Sergeant Joe Zolinski of the First Canadian Division. He had been captured when he had run into a column of German panzers during some heavy fighting around Pontecorvo and had ended up in the same prisoner-of-war camp. Like his English comrade, he still bore the marks of exhaustion. He was tall, deeply sunburned and would have had an athletic build if the months of captivity had not taken their toll. Constanza had a swift impression of light grey eyes set in a haggard, unshaven young face. He broke into a wide grin. "They treated us OK, more or less," he said. "The food was pretty terrible, but the boredom was worse – caged up all the time with nothing to look at but barbed wire. David and I were in the same hut. We played a hell of a lot of chess – he's not much good at it but I'm worse."

"You can say that again," said David.

"It was when the rumour got out that we were going to be moved north to another camp in Germany that I got seriously scared. Well, we all did – but I'm half Jewish. Never bothered me before. Why should it? My dad died when I was a kid and my mom's French-Canadian, so I was brought up a Catholic, like her. But it's the Jewish surname that registers with these Fascists. Even if you go to Mass every Sunday they still get suspicious."

"Camps in Germany are a lot tougher," added David. "So we knew if we wanted to escape it was now or never."

"How did you manage it?" asked Constanza.

"It was the Partisans who helped spring us," Joe told her. "They've got contacts, those boys. I got a message inside a bread roll. Don't ask me how they got it in there. It told me they could get two of our guys out, me and one other, so I picked David. Seems like I'm fated to be stuck with him." They exchanged comradely grins in the dark.

"They told us to act normal and be on the alert," Joe went on. "Mostly we were kept in the camp, only allowed in the exercise yard at certain times. But sometimes some of us were taken out on working parties. Mending roads, that sort of stuff – under guard, of course. So we were out digging ditches on a stretch of road near a field of maize and there was this scarecrow stuck up there – old raggedy coat, battered hat, straw hair and all. Except it wasn't a scarecrow. There was a guy inside who started firing at us with a rifle. Just a few shots – missed us, of course, he wasn't trying to hit us, but it sure grabbed the attention of our guards. They were yelling at each other in German and firing back, and in all the commotion, this other guy appeared out of nowhere and got us away. We ran like hell up a track behind an olive grove and into the woods before they noticed we were gone. The guy in the scarecrow managed to get away too – can't think how he did it. They seem to know how to kind of melt into the landscape."

"They took us on foot through the mountains and we've been hiding out with them until they arranged to bring us here," David told her. "It was hard being with the Partisans. They're a pretty tough lot. There's a guy in charge – the one who contacted you – but they're not all buddies, or in total agreement with each other. Far from it. There's a lot of tension between them. Some of them hate the Communists, the Reds. But they are holding together at least until our chaps liberate Florence."

"Which will be soon?" asked Constanza.

Joe shrugged. "Who knows for sure. I guess so. I sure want to be back with my outfit before it happens, though."

CHAPTER 12

For Rosemary, sitting upstairs in her room, the day was dragging by interminably. She was attempting to relieve the tension by writing to her mother; a letter which she knew was extremely unlikely ever to arrive. Postal communication between Italy and England, two countries at war, was totally unreliable.

"We are all well here and managing to avoid food shortages somehow," she wrote, "I do hope it's the same for you, Mummy, and you're not getting too exhausted with all the work you're doing for the war effort."

She paused.

Why am I writing this kind of bracing, optimistic stuff when I know she'll probably never read it? she thought. *Mind you, I never did tell her anything about what's really happening to me, anyway.*

The old pre-war England she remembered was becoming a kind of faraway edifice of her own memories, and her mother was rapidly becoming part of it.

When her father had died, in 1938, it had been one of the great sadnesses of Rosemary's life, a loss from which she would never fully recover. She had seen so little of him in the years since her marriage. There had been visits to London with the children, of course, mostly without Franco, who had been too busy to accompany them. Her father had been deeply worried about the rise of Fascism in Europe and the inevitability of another war. For his generation, having witnessed the carnage in the trenches during the First World War, it was an unthinkable dread. She had watched his old sociable optimism turn to gloomy introspection and his health decline as a result. And when he had died suddenly of a heart attack, she had not been there.

Once war had been declared against Britain, Rosemary, who was living in Florence and married to an Italian, could have little contact with her

English mother, though she guessed that she would be surviving widowhood with her characteristic brisk energy. War work would provide her with an ideal opportunity to overcome her grief. When the bombing had begun in earnest, Rosemary had pictured her mother channelling all her formidable organizational skills into helping to evacuate London children and running canteens for servicemen and -women and hostels for bombed-out families.

The rare letters that had got through from her had been full of buoyant enthusiasm. Her mother's only complaint was that the deafening nightly barrage from the big anti-aircraft guns on Primrose Hill was robbing her of a decent night's sleep.

If only I could be more like her, thought Rosemary. *I'd give anything to be so single-minded.*

Her own position in Florence demanded a different kind of bravery, though. It was a lonely life of waiting, keeping a low profile and trying to protect her children. And it was all falling apart. She seemed to have lost control altogether, and all she could think was that she had put her family in mortal danger.

She buried her face in her hands. *Oh, Franco,* she thought, *if only you were here*.

*   *   *

Paolo, meanwhile, was hanging about the house in a state of high excitement, finding it impossible to settle to anything. He just wanted the action to start. The trip to Florence was planned for just after dark when, with luck, there would not be too many military police patrols around. His stomach turned over with fear every time he thought about what he had agreed to do. But there was no going back now. He had checked his bicycle three times already that morning and he was ready. At last he was going to get some action, a real man's job. Helping Allied servicemen escape was really something special, something he could tell his father about when he came home, even if he could never let on about it to his friends.

He hovered about in the hall at the top of the cellar stairs. Why was Constanza taking so long down there? What were they talking about? He wondered if he should go down and join them but then thought better of it. Perhaps he should keep a low profile for the moment.

Constanza finally appeared, carrying two empty plates.

"You've been a long time," said Paolo. "Are

they OK? What have they been telling you about themselves?"

But Constanza, he could see, was in one of her maddeningly uncommunicative moods.

"Not much," was all she would say. "One's Canadian Army and the other's RAF. I really don't know much more than that."

But Paolo was pretty sure that she did and that she was just as full of suppressed excitement as he was.

"Didn't they tell you…?" he began, but stopped short. Somebody was moving about in the drawing room.

Then a voice called, "Hello? Anyone at home?"

Hilaria! They exchanged horrified looks. She had come in unannounced through the French windows and was wandering nosily around. She strolled into the hall to join them, immaculately dressed as usual in a crisp linen suit.

"Only me," she said brightly. "I hope it's all right my barging in like this. I had to get out for a bit – it's so boring at home, so I just thought I'd drop by to see what you're doing. I wondered if perhaps we could listen to some of your records, Constanza. But if you're madly busy…"

"No, not at all," said Constanza.

Hilaria glanced sharply at the two plates Constanza was carrying, then at the cellar door. Paolo saw to his horror that it had been left half open. Constanza caught his eye. She reached back with her foot and kicked the door shut, but she was a split second too late. Hilaria laughed.

"So, since when have you and Paolo taken to eating your lunch in the cellar?" she said.

"Oh, we've just been helping Maria do a bit of clearing-up down there. It's so full of junk."

"Fascinating! I just adore junk. You never know what treasures you're going to find. Food as well, it seems. You must let me nose around there sometime."

"Sure, but not in that white suit, Hilaria," said Constanza, thinking quickly. "It's terribly dusty down there. Let's go up to my room."

But Hilaria seemed in no hurry to leave the hall and began wandering about, idly picking things up and putting them down again.

"It's chaos at home," she said. "Too depressing for words! Packing cases everywhere. Mamma and Papà don't feel safe in Florence any longer and we're planning to go to Lake Como, if we can manage to get there. But Aldo doesn't want to leave. He's got all sorts of deals going with the German administration here and he's worried he'll miss out on the money they owe him. He's such a good businessman, you know. I don't really want to leave either, to be honest. Mamma says there's only room for one suitcase each in the car and that means leaving most of my clothes behind. Can you imagine having to choose what to take! It's too awful."

"I can't believe that you'll be very popular here when the Allies arrive," said Paolo.

"You don't know anything about it," said Hilaria coolly, "so don't pretend that you do."

"Oh, come on upstairs," Constanza put in quickly.

They were halfway up the first flight when they heard a muffled noise from the cellar. Hilaria paused and looked back.

"It sounds as if Maria could do with some help down there," she said. But at that moment Maria herself bustled into the hallway from the kitchen, making it plain that if anyone was down there in the cellar, it wasn't her.

CHAPTER 13

Hilaria stayed for nearly two hours. Paolo hardly knew how they got through her highly unwelcome visit. Reluctantly, he had to admire the cool way Constanza dealt with the situation. She had managed somehow to laugh off Hilaria's curiosity about what had gone bump in the cellar, saying that they must have piled up so much junk that it had toppled over and – *oh dear!* – they would probably have to start clearing up again later. Fortunately, it was Hilaria's unwillingness to get her white suit dirty that finally made her lose interest.

After Constanza had managed to manoeuvre her upstairs and Paolo heard the familiar sound of the gramophone playing "J'attendrai", he flopped down on the drawing-room sofa, feeling quite sick with relief.

Hilaria finally left at about four o'clock. After that there was nothing for any of them to do except wait until dark. It was around nine when Constanza crept down to fetch Joe and David from the cellar and brought them out to join Paolo in the yard. They were wearing caps pulled well down over their faces and each carried a canvas bag slung over his shoulder like any Italian man returning late from work. They had already said a brief, grateful goodbye to Rosemary. Now the two men, Paolo and Constanza stood there, shy and at a loss for words.

"We'll try to let you know somehow where we end up," said Joe, looking at Constanza.

"Send you a picture postcard," added David.

"Take care," said Constanza. It seemed wholly inadequate, but it was the best she could manage. She put her arms around each of them in turn and hugged them. She was taken by surprise by the warmth with which Joe returned her embrace. She wondered why the fate of these two young men, whom she had known for less than twenty-four hours, suddenly meant so much to her. *Why am I always saying goodbye?* she thought sadly, reminded of her father's long absence.

Paolo was impatient to be off. Silently, and determined not to let on how nervous he was, he led the two men down the back drive towards the road. Rosemary was standing alone in the kitchen, unable to bear watching them go.

Their journey downhill towards the city was uneventful. The houses showed no chink of light. Very few people ventured out after dark now even before the curfew and those who had took little notice of them. But as they approached the Porta Romana Paolo's heart sank. A German military patrol was parked by the roadside and four soldiers were stopping people at random. Paolo tried to pass by unnoticed but one of the men, a corporal, motioned to them at gunpoint to stop.

"Passes? Show your passes," he said in broken Italian.

Joe and David stood well back, heads down, as they fumbled in their jackets. The single carefully shaded light from the soldier's torch threw their shadows out across the street. Paolo stepped forward, offering his own papers and rallying all his linguistic skills to speak to the man in German.

"They're from out of town," he said, jerking his head at his two companions. "They're from the North, near Brescia. Been working near here in a munitions factory. I'm local. I'm taking them into town to stay the night with a relative. Then they're going to work their way back home if they can."

The corporal relaxed slightly at the sound of his own language.

"You're a bit young to be out at night," he said, eyeing Paolo. "Make sure you're back inside before the curfew begins."

"I'm OK. I know my way around. I've got my bicycle and I'm going straight home after this."

The soldier glanced at Joe and David and motioned for them to show their passes, which he scrutinized under his torch. Then he told them to walk on.

They did so in silence and did not relax until they were some way down the Via Romana into the city. Paolo could see the sweat on Joe's face. They passed the Angelina Convent and crossed the deserted Piazza de' Pitti, where the great looming shape of the Pitti Palace rose high above them, all its windows dark.

As they approached the river, Paolo led the way into a side street to the right. He wanted to avoid crossing the Ponte Vecchio in case they ran into another checkpoint there. Instead, they took a roundabout route that came out onto the Lungarno Torrigiani, the road that bordered the river on the south side, and crossed safely to the north side over the Ponte alle Grazie. Then they plunged into the network of little streets near the Santa Croce.

Paolo had studied the route. He knew these streets well from his night rides – knew every doorway and alley they could dodge into if they were spotted. But all they encountered were one or two heavily laden women, intent on getting back to their houses as quickly as possible, and a few half-starved cats. At last they reached the end of a very long, narrow and deserted street. It was in almost complete darkness and all the houses were closely shuttered.

"It's number seventeen," whispered David. "I'll go first and then I'll signal for you both to follow."

He walked lightly and rapidly, until he came to a door at the far end of the street. He knocked twice. At first, there was no response, only what seemed like an interminable pause. Then suddenly the door was flung open, and in the rectangle of light that spilled out onto the street Paolo could see soldiers – German soldiers. They grabbed David, pinning his arms behind his back.

"It's a trap! Run!" he shouted before they silenced him with a blow.

There was a lot of shouting then and confusion. A bullet hit the wall behind Paolo's head. The plaster shattered and fell to the ground, but he was too stunned to be frightened. He reacted blindly, without hesitation.

"This way," he said, pulling Joe along with one hand and clutching his bicycle with the other. Two more shots followed as they made their way off around the corner. He felt Joe stumble and fall against him, but Joe quickly righted himself and kept running. Other doors were being flung open now and people were coming out into the street: women were screaming; men were gesticulating. The panic that ensued gave them a few seconds' lead. Paolo pulled Joe into a side alleyway which led through to another street. It was then that he remembered the ice-cream shop.

Ice creams were a long-forgotten dream, a memory of happy afternoons before the war:

shopping with his mother followed by delicious treats. His favourite place to go had been the ice-cream shop. The parlour had closed when the war began but he recognized the door and remembered how the kindly proprietor had once shown him the big refrigerators containing the different flavoured ices. He gave the back door a push. It creaked open. Quickly, he shoved his bicycle inside and then, after dragging Joe inside, shut the door behind them. He could hear running footsteps very close at hand – booted feet on cobbles – and orders shouted in German. Joe and Paolo stood together in the half-dark. Joe was leaning heavily on him, heaving for breath. Paolo gripped his arm and encountered something warm and sticky – blood.

"They got me in the shoulder with that second shot," Joe whispered hoarsely.

Paolo was too scared to answer. Instead, he looked around. It was the ice-cream shop, all right. They seemed to be in the kitchen. It smelt of damp, decay and urine but there they were the two big fridges looming up out of the dark. Outside, the soldiers were kicking open doors all along the alley. Paolo shoved his bicycle into a corner and pulled Joe behind one of the fridges. There was just room for them, if they pressed up against the wall.

A second later the door from the alleyway was flung open and two soldiers burst in. Torches flashed around the room, packing cases were pulled aside and cupboards searched. Both fridge doors were wrenched open. Paolo held his breath. One man was so near to him that he could have reached out and touched Paolo's arm.

Then one of the soldiers spotted the bicycle. There was an exchange and the door that lead into the shop was kicked open. The soldiers rushed through, rifles at the ready.

"Come on," whispered Paolo. He grabbed the bike and he and Joe slipped out silently into the alley. Paolo peered down the street. He could hear excited voices near by, but in the immediate vicinity there was nobody about and all was quiet. He motioned for Joe to follow him but, looking back, he saw that Joe was not in a good way. He was staggering, and blood had soaked through the left arm of his jacket and was dripping down his hand. Paolo ran back to him. Somehow he managed to support the wounded man as far as the bicycle and lever him onto the seat.

"It's OK. Hang on to me," he said.

Then, with Joe clinging onto his waist with his good arm, Paolo shoved off. He cycled hard, standing high on the pedals, and within minutes they were away up the darkened street.

The way home was the worst journey Paolo had ever made. He took the back streets out of the city, dreading at every turn that they would run into another German patrol. Joe was tall and broad, and he seemed a dead-weight to Paolo, who was finding it almost impossible to support him, even along the flat. As they began their ascent up the road towards home Paolo had to dismount and push his bicycle, with Joe slumped upon it.

It was hard-going. They went on in silence, with Paolo heaving for breath. They were both thinking of David and how they had had to abandon him to his fate at the hands of his German captors. They had run out on him – they both knew that all too clearly, though they also knew that any attempt to save him would have been futile and would probably have resulted in all three of them being captured or shot. Paolo tried to concentrate on reaching home. It was the only thing that mattered now.

CHAPTER 14

Rosemary and Constanza were sitting huddled together at the kitchen table when, at last, they heard the crunch of bicycle wheels in the yard. The waiting had been a mounting agony for Rosemary. She had steeled herself to keeping watch for Paolo for a couple of hours, but when midnight had passed and he had not returned her anxiety turned to cold panic.

She had been outside several times and walked as far as the road, peering into the darkness in the hope of seeing that shaded bicycle lamp wavering up the hill. But all was silent and empty. When Constanza had crept downstairs to join her, Rosemary was far too grateful for the company to insist that she should go back to bed. It helped to have a hand to hold.

"Why did I ever let him get into this? It's my fault entirely. I should never have allowed it," Rosemary kept repeating.

"Don't worry, Mamma. He'll be back."

But as time wore on even these exchanges had petered out and they were reduced to silence.

The moment they heard Paolo in the yard, they both rushed outside. He had flung down his bicycle and was half dragging, half supporting Joe towards the back door. Rosemary's enormous relief at seeing him safe home overrode her shock at the sight of Joe with his arm soaked in blood. It was Constanza who had to stand still, pressing her hands to her mouth to stop herself from crying out.

Almost within seconds, Rosemary had moved to take control of the situation with calm efficiency, hoping that nobody would notice how much she was trembling. Somehow, between the three of them, they managed to get Joe into the kitchen, where he fell into a chair, barely conscious, with his head slumped onto his chest. Paolo, white-faced with exhaustion, stood leaning against the doorway, talking rapidly but making very little sense. The words poured out incoherently as, between gulps, he tried to describe what had happened.

"David – they got David," he kept saying.

Rosemary put an arm around him, holding him very tightly and trying to calm him.

"All right, *caro* – all right. Sit down a moment and we'll hear about it later. Constanza, will you put the kettle on and fetch the first-aid box from my bathroom as quickly as you can? And for heaven's sake, don't wake Maria! She'll only get in a terrible state and make matters worse."

When Constanza returned with the box, Joe was lying on the sofa in the drawing room. Rosemary carefully began to cut away the sleeve of his jacket and blood-soaked shirt. Then she gently sponged away some of the blood from around his wound.

"It's a bad gash," she said. "But it doesn't look as though there's a bullet hole. It must have grazed your arm but just missed going in, thank heavens."

Joe had revived enough to sip some hot tea laced with a little brandy and Rosemary began to dress his shoulder. As she worked, he and Paolo described their night's adventure. Paolo was calmer now.

When the bandage was on, Joe lay back exhausted.

"Looks as though I've fetched up here again like a dud nickel," he said with a weak grin, "but don't worry, I'll get away again somehow…"

"Is it possible you could be traced back here, do you think?" asked Rosemary anxiously.

"We weren't followed, I'm pretty sure of that," said Paolo. "If we had been, they would have caught up with us long before we got back here."

Rosemary pressed her hands to her forehead, struggling to remain calm, or at least not to let her panic show. She had no idea what to do next.

"I can't get a doctor for you, Joe. It's far too risky," she said. "Nobody outside this household must know what's happened. We're very suspect here. But you can't possibly go on the run in this state."

"I won't let you risk having me here any longer," said Joe. "The Partisans will be in contact. They'll get me away somehow…"

"Not until you've rested and got over the shock," said Rosemary. "We'll hide you in the cellar. Nobody will suspect anything if we lie low and act as normally as possible."

Joe tried to rally the energy to insist but he was too tired.

"I keep thinking about David – what they'll do to the poor guy. We ran away and left him…" Joe screwed up his face in agony.

"From what you say there wasn't much else you could do, except get taken yourselves or be shot," said Constanza.

"Yeah, I know, I know." Joe reached out his good hand to Paolo. "You were great, kid, just great. They'd have got me too if it hadn't been for you. You're a whole heap braver than most of the army guys I know, and that's for sure."

Suddenly, Paolo covered his face with his hands and began to weep. Rosemary held him tightly.

"Right now, what we all need is some sleep," she said.

CHAPTER 15

They were awoken late the following morning by the ominous sound of gunfire coming from the hills north of Florence. It sounded as though the fighting was getting ever nearer to the city. Maria was in a particularly unmanageable state of panic mixed with stubborn bad temper and she slammed around the kitchen, muttering dire warnings. Joe was still asleep in the cellar, but she refused to go down there or have anything to do with the *"Americano"*, as she called him, insisting that he would get them all shot.

It was Constanza who went down to wake him and take his breakfast. He was almost too exhausted to eat and just wanted to drift in and out of sleep.

"Poor Joe – it's so dark and stuffy down there,"

Constanza said to her mother when she came back upstairs; "and it smells of damp."

"It'll begin to smell of Joe, too, before long," said Paolo, chewing a roll, his spirits and appetite now fully restored.

"It's too risky for him to come out, not even into the yard," said Rosemary. "There are German troops on the move everywhere."

"I can try to find the Partisans," said Paolo. "I've got my bicycle."

But Rosemary was adamantly against any such suggestion. "I absolutely forbid you to leave the house, Paolo, and that's final. You could put us all in danger, maybe even get us arrested. We'll just have to hang on until they contact us. They'll get in touch somehow."

But, as it turned out, it was not the Partisans but the police who broke the silence that hung over the house that day. Around noon the telephone rang. Rosemary answered.

"*Signora* Crivelli? This is Captain Spinetti of the *carabinieri*. Is it possible to have a private word with you? I must be brief."

"Of course, Captain."

"Both your children are at home?"

"Yes – we've been told to keep indoors. We have enough food to last for a day or two."

"Good. I thought I might warn you – in absolute confidence, you understand…" He lowered his voice. "You know, of course, that the Gestapo are very active here, based in my office."

"Yes, I know."

"Colonel Richter came in early this morning. The German military authorities have informed us that there was an incident in the city last night. An escaped prisoner of war was captured, but another got away."

"Really? We hadn't heard…"

"The one who escaped was not alone. He had an accomplice – a boy on a bicycle."

There was a long pause.

"*Signora* Crivelli? Are you still there?"

"Yes, I'm here."

The captain's voice dropped still further.

"Of course you realize that it's highly irregular for me to telephone you like this. The city is under military law and – as you know – it's a capital offence for Italian civilians to aid the enemy in any way."

"I know."

"As we are old friends, I thought I might mention that you may have an official visit from the Gestapo later today. Someone has mentioned your name to them as being possibly suspect. So if you need to prepare in any way…"

"I understand, Captain. Please don't say any more. And thank you. I'm so very grateful."

When she rang off, Rosemary had to hold on to the edge of the table to steady herself. Her legs hardly seemed able to support her.

"Franco – oh, Franco – what am I going to do now?" she said aloud. But she knew she was talking to an empty room.

Her first coherent thought was that she must rouse Joe and warn him of this imminent danger, however frail he might be feeling. But before that she had to make some sort of plan.

She summoned Paolo and Constanza, and the three of them huddled around the kitchen table, talking in urgent whispers, although there was nobody to overhear them.

"They could be here at any time," said Rosemary, "and they'll be sure to search the cellar. We'll have to hide Joe somewhere else right away – get him out of the house altogether if possible."

"Could we hide him in the garden, or in the barn?" suggested Constanza.

"No – they'll be sure to search there too. They're nothing if not thorough."

"I could get him to the hillside on the back of my bicycle," said Paolo. "He could lie low out there until the coast's clear."

Rosemary shook her head vehemently.

"I don't think that's possible, Paolo. Joe's in a very poor state and he's lost a lot of blood. How would you manage if he collapsed completely?"

"There must be somewhere we can hide him," Paolo said suddenly. "Wait a minute – I know! What about the little wine store under the grating right next to the cellar? The one I… I mean, the one nobody would think of unless they actually knew it was there."

Rosemary's mind was racing.

"It might do," she said. "We've got to be quick, though. Do you think we can disguise the door that leads from the cellar? And the trapdoor from outside?"

"You bet," said Paolo.

"Right. Maria's better left out of this, so, Paolo, can you begin covering up the outside? There's that pile of old wine crates in the yard. You can put them on top of the trapdoor and scatter some grass cuttings around. Constanza, you'd better come down to the cellar with me. We've got to break it to Joe and get the place completely cleared up – we can't leave a sign of anyone having been in there. We must hurry!"

Joe was dazed when they woke him, but he grasped the situation very quickly and tried as best he could with his good arm to help Rosemary roll up all the bedding and hide it under a pile of old curtains. Constanza was pulling away all the piles of junk around the little door that led to the wine store.

"Check the air holes in this door," Rosemary told her, "and put a bottle of water and a couple of blankets in there. Oh, and my electric torch."

They worked frantically, ears strained for the sound of approaching cars. Above, they could hear Paolo at work piling up loose grass cuttings over the trapdoor and dragging the wine crates from the yard.

"It's terribly uncomfortable, I'm afraid," said Constanza.

"Don't worry, I'll be OK," Joe said as he stooped to get inside. He folded his long legs against the upturned box that they had put in there for him to sit on.

"Are you sure you've got enough air?" asked Constanza anxiously as she closed the door on him.

"Sure. And it's real kind of you to do this for me…" came the muffled voice from inside.

The next task was to reassemble the assorted junk, old trunks and suitcases, cartons of broken electrical equipment and discarded magazines, so that nobody could guess the door was there. Finally, Constanza placed the tailor's dummy dressed in her grandfather's old uniform in front of the door to create what she hoped was a diversion, while Rosemary swept the dusty floor clear of footprints. Then they both ran upstairs to wash, change and comb their hair.

CHAPTER 16

Rosemary, Constanza and Paolo were sitting in the drawing room, attempting to appear relaxed, when they heard the sound of vehicles drawing up outside. There was an authoritative knock at the front door. Rosemary put aside her sewing and went to answer it. Three men in civilian dress – Gestapo – one of whom was Colonel Richter, stood on the doorstep. Parked on the drive behind his car was an army truck containing two German soldiers and an officer, who jumped out and saluted. It was Lieutenant Gräss.

"*Buona sera, Signora* Crivelli—" he began politely, but the colonel cut him off abruptly.

"*Signora* Crivelli? I am Colonel Richter, attached

to the civilian police here in Florence."

"I know. Captain Spinetti has spoken of you."

"Possibly he has. As you know, the city and surrounding area are now under martial law. You may have heard that there was an incident with two prisoners of war last night. One of them was apprehended but the other got away."

"I hadn't heard. We – my son and daughter and our one servant, Maria – have been confined to the house. We haven't been out, not even to buy food."

"You are British, I think?"

"Yes, by birth. But I have been an Italian citizen for many years now. My passport and all my papers are in order, if you would care to see them?"

He ignored this and went on, "We have orders to search your property."

"Certainly. Won't you come in?" Rosemary stood back to allow them to enter. Lieutenant Gräss signalled to the soldiers, who followed him inside. Colonel Richter gave orders for the house and gardens to be searched and then followed Rosemary into the drawing room, where Paolo and Constanza were waiting. Rosemary invited the colonel to sit down, an offer which was curtly refused. Constanza,

Rosemary and Paolo then sat in strained silence, listening to the sounds of the search progressing overhead; heavy boots crossed the floor, cupboards were flung open and furniture was pulled about.

Meanwhile, Richter stalked restlessly up and down. Soon they heard the sound of Maria scolding the soldiers shrilly at the top of her voice. She was abruptly and threateningly ordered back to the kitchen. She retreated, muttering, and slammed the door. At last, after a long agony of waiting, both search parties reassembled in the hall, along with Rosemary, Paolo and Constanza. Lieutenant Gräss reported that nothing unusual had been found in the house or grounds.

"Do you have a cellar?" Richter asked Rosemary.

Only Paolo and Constanza noticed the slight tightening of her throat as she indicated the door.

"Down those stairs. We use it for storing junk. There's no electric light down there, I'm afraid. Constanza, run and get an oil lamp, will you?"

Richter signalled to Gräss with an abrupt jerk of his head. The lieutenant led the way down into the cellar and two soldiers clumped down after him, shining their electric torches. Constanza followed them and set the lamp down on an upturned packing case. She leant against the wall at the foot of the stairs. The uniformed dummy threw up a looming shadow against the tottering pile of junk which masked Joe's hiding place.

Please, please don't look behind it, Constanza prayed silently, but outwardly, with a great effort of will, she maintained a slightly bored indifference.

The two soldiers, under Lieutenant Gräss's direction, were very thorough. Working their way steadily across the room, they investigated boxes, piles of old clothing and discarded household appliances, shifting them around to make sure that nobody was hiding behind or under them. Gräss, meanwhile, was shining a torch into corners and carefully examining the floor.

Thank heavens we swept away all the footprints, thought Constanza. Then she saw the lieutenant stop short and kneel down. He picked something up and held it under the lamp to examine it more closely. She was near enough to see that it was part of an old cigarette packet. The printing on it was clearly legible: LUCKY STRIKE. An American brand.

It must have fallen out of Joe's pocket, thought

Constanza with a lurch of fear in her stomach. *Oh, how could I have missed it when I was sweeping up?*

Gräss was looking at the floor again, very carefully indeed. He straightened up and examined the paper once more. Then his eyes met Constanza's very briefly. She looked back at him with a direct, level gaze, praying that the flush she could feel rising from her neck to her face was not visible in the lamplight. He paused before crushing the scrap of paper into a tiny ball and dropping it behind one of the boxes. He never once glanced at her again, but she noticed that he was hurrying his men on. They only had time for a perfunctory search around the entrance to Joe's hiding place before he ordered them to return upstairs. Constanza followed, carrying the lamp, her face now carefully arranged in an expression as non-committal as Gräss's own. Nobody could have guessed, as the party reassembled in the hall, how fast her heart was beating.

Colonel Richter tapped his gloves against the table in the hall with ill-concealed irritation as Gräss reported that nothing had been found. There were a few brusque exchanges between them and then Richter summoned his two plain-clothes Gestapo men, who had been waiting outside, bowed stiffly to Rosemary and, ignoring Constanza and Paolo altogether, stalked out to his car.

As soon as he had driven off, followed closely by Gräss and his party in the army truck, Rosemary, Constanza and Paolo bolted back down the cellar stairs. There was no time to spare – they had to clear away the junk and free Joe from his stifling hiding place.

"It's all right, Joe – it's only us!" called Constanza softly, but there was no reply. When at last they got the little door open, they found Joe half conscious and dripping with sweat. Paolo dragged a mattress back onto the floor and Constanza and Rosemary half supported, half carried him out. The first thing he did was to be violently sick. Constanza ran for a bowl, a sponge and a glass of water. Joe came round after a few sips, and drank greedily. Then he lay back while Rosemary cleaned him up and put a fresh dressing on his shoulder wound.

He tried to smile but was too exhausted to manage it. "Gee, I'm sorry about all this. I'm... It's..." He failed to finish the sentence. He was already asleep, his good arm flung across his face like a kid afraid of the dark.

Upstairs, Rosemary made a pot of tea and put out what was left of the day's meagre bread ration. It was still only late afternoon, hot and sunny outside, but as the three of them sat there, gulping and chewing but otherwise in silence, it seemed as though they had come to the end of a very long day.

CHAPTER 17

There was very little rest for any of them that night. Joe, who was still sleeping, exhausted, in the cellar, was the only one not to be kept awake by the noise of shelling and gunfire growing ever closer. German troops were moving up the road outside – armoured cars, tanks and truckloads of soldiers – travelling to the front line, which was now not far away.

Paolo got up very early while it was still only half light and wandered out into the yard. He felt the need for Guido's company and the old dog's unfailing, unquestioning loyalty. He found him dozing half in and half out of his kennel. The dog lumbered to his feet when he heard Paolo and wagged his tail, not yet so old that he could not manage a warm welcome.

Paolo knelt down beside him and absently fondled his ears. In spite of his own weariness, he was thinking hard, wondering what on earth would happen to the family now. He was very frightened and kept listening for the sound of Colonel Richter's car. He knew that if the search party returned – as they easily might – and found Joe, it would mean not only the Canadian's recapture but his mother's arrest for hiding him. And with Florence under martial law, they could both be summarily shot without trial.

A huge anger welled up in Paolo. It was directed, quite irrationally, against Joe for "fetching up" back in their cellar. And there was the old anger, too, the one against his father for not being there to protect them, for putting his political convictions first and the family second. Why, oh why, wasn't he here? All the bravado and excitement Paolo had felt the other night when he had insisted on being Joe and David's guide into Florence seemed foolhardy, a crazy kid's game. Since the terrible moment when he had heard that German bullet hit the wall behind his head – a sound that would be replayed over and over in his worst dreams for ever – he had known for sure that this was no game.

If only I could get in touch with Babbo, he thought desperately for the hundredth time. *If there were some way I could get a message to him. Surely then he'd come back and take charge. He'd know what to do.*

But it was hopeless. Not even his mother knew where his father was hiding – that knowledge was too dangerous.

Guido was resting his slobbery jaw on Paolo's knee, hoping for something to eat. Paolo found a morsel of bread in his pocket and gave it to him. He checked that the water bowl at least was full. He was thinking hard. There was only one thing to be done, he decided. They couldn't afford to wait for the Partisans to come to them. He had to try to contact them and get them to take Joe back into hiding somewhere in the hills. Then perhaps Il Volpe himself would be able to find a way to get him to safety.

He stood up and glanced at the house. Nobody was up and about yet, not even Maria. He had to act now, before his courage failed him. Giving a last affectionate tug to Guido's ears, he walked quickly to the shed where he kept his bicycle.

He headed towards the place where he had encountered Il Volpe and his fellow Partisans for the first time. As he rode, he heard the sound of explosions, followed by machine gunfire. Both were frighteningly near. But he kept going. He rode for about half an hour. When the track again became too steep he dismounted and began to push his bicycle as he had before. He thought he recognized some of the turns he had taken not so long ago when he had thought that coming up here was such an adventure. A hero on a bicycle, as he had seen himself then. This time he was just plain scared.

He suddenly stopped and listened. He could hear sounds of movement coming from beyond the next bend. Somebody was approaching. He quickly dragged his bicycle into the bushes and crouched down beside it.

A posse of four German soldiers, helmeted and in full military kit, rifles at the ready, came around the corner. Paolo's heart contracted with fear. In their midst stumbled a figure he knew well. It was Il Volpe himself.

CHAPTER 18

As soon as she was awake, Constanza softly descended to the cellar, carrying Joe's breakfast: a cup of hot milk and a dry roll (the family butter ration had run out days ago). It was horribly stuffy, so she left the door at the top of the stairs open to let in some air and a little light. She found him still drowsy but recovered enough to scramble up into a sitting position as soon as he saw her.

"Sleep all right?" she asked.

"Yeah – like the dead. Which is probably what I would be now if it hadn't been for you and your mom and Paolo, and what you did for me yesterday."

"Not you, Joe. You're a – what's the word? – a survivor." She smiled and handed him the cup. They sat side by side on the mattress. He sipped in silence for a while, and then he said, "I've got to get out of here, right now. I can't let you put yourselves on the line for me any longer. It's too dangerous. Those Gestapo swine could come back again any time."

"But where will you go?"

"If I can, I'll make it into the hills. I'll be all right. It can't be long before this city gets liberated. The fighting's really close now." As if to reinforce his words, they heard a sudden burst of gunfire not so far away. Constanza jumped.

Joe looked at her. "You're too young to be mixed up in all this," he said. "You ought to be – I don't know – somewhere wonderful, having a good time. Not stuck here, having to be so brave."

"Not brave," said Constanza. Her voice wobbled. "Not brave at all."

Joe put down his cup. He reached out his good arm and took her hand. She held on to him tightly. They sat like that for a while without speaking. Then Joe took her face in both his hands.

"Brave," he said again, "and beautiful, too." His face was sad and almost puzzled in the half-dark. He began to stroke her hair, very gently, pushing it away from her forehead. Somehow, rather awkwardly, their faces grew very close together. Constanza closed her eyes…

"Paolo! Paolo, are you down there?" Maria's raucous voice came from the top of the stairs. "Constanza?" she called again. "Is Paolo there? Constanza! Have you seen him?"

"He's not down here," Constanza answered wearily.

Rosemary was in the kitchen, already dressed but looking white-faced and strained.

"We need food," she said when Constanza came in carrying Joe's empty cup. "There's hardly any left. Maria and I will see if we can get down to the farm the back way, through the garden. It's too dangerous on the road. How's Joe?"

Constanza was in no mood for conversation. "Better, I think," she said briefly, then added, "He's talking about trying to hide out somewhere in the hills."

"It's too soon yet. He needs another day's rest before he's fit to try it."

Maria was fiddling irritatingly with the radio,

attempting to get the BBC European service or Voice of America. When at last she managed it they caught something about the Allied invasion of Northern France and the liberation of Cherbourg by the Americans, but nothing about the progress of the war in Italy. They must have missed it.

"We should go," said Rosemary, switching off the wireless. "Constanza, you and Paolo mustn't go out on any account. Where *is* Paolo anyway? He can't have been so silly as to have gone wandering off somewhere – he must know how dangerous it is."

"He's probably mooching around in the garden," said Constanza. "I'll go and look."

While she was gone, Rosemary went out into the yard. For the moment, the road outside was deserted and there seemed to be a lull in the nerve-racking noise of shelling. She hurried round to the bicycle shed and looked inside.

"Oh, no!" she said aloud when she saw that Paolo's bicycle was missing. "Oh, Paolo – please – no!"

CHAPTER 19

Paolo held his breath as the German soldiers and their prisoner passed. Il Volpe's hands were roped behind his back and his face was badly bruised. One eye was almost closed and there was a gaping cut on his forehead which was bleeding down into his beard.

Paolo waited tensely until they had gone on ahead. He then crept out of the bushes and began to follow at a safe distance, wheeling his bicycle and keeping well in the shadow of the trees, ready to dodge out of sight at any moment. They kept going for some time along the narrow track until it forked – they took the wider path going steeply downhill in the opposite direction to the way Paolo had come. He was getting further and further away from home, and he had no clear idea what he hoped to achieve, but he kept on going.

Occasionally Il Volpe stumbled and fell but the soldiers kicked him until he was back on his feet again.

The track became a dirt road. Soon there were dry-stone walls, and the trees gave way to olive groves, vineyards and the occasional group of farm buildings, baking in the noonday heat. It became almost impossible for Paolo to follow without being spotted. He let them go out of sight and turned into a farm track. He threw down his bicycle and sprawled on the ground beside it. He felt completely lost. And only now did he realize how terrified he was.

He wondered what had happened to the other Partisans. Perhaps they were all dead, or maybe they were not even aware that Il Volpe had been captured. Where were those German soldiers taking him? Wherever it was, Paolo thought, there was nothing he could do to help him now.

Suddenly, out of nowhere, three German fighter planes – Messerschmitts – ripped through the sky overhead and there was a burst of heavy gunfire not far away. Paolo automatically ducked down and covered his head with his hands. More than anything in the world, he wanted to get back home. The best way, he thought, was to follow the road to a village and try to make it back from there. Wearily, and aching with hunger and thirst, he lugged his bicycle back onto the road and set off.

The nearest village was much further away than he had calculated. En route, he was overtaken by a couple of army trucks full of German soldiers with rifles at the ready. They roared past in a cloud of dust and nearly tipped him into the ditch. At last he reached the outskirts of a village and entered one of the narrow streets that led down to the church and the main piazza. In spite of it being siesta time and stiflingly hot, there were a great many people about. They stood silent and watchful on their doorsteps or in huddled groups, murmuring anxiously. They looked at him warily as he cycled past, but he kept his eyes on the street. Then, thank heavens, he found a wall fountain. He dismounted and took a long, long drink and then doused his head under the running water. It was wonderfully, deliciously cool. He sat there for a few minutes, letting his aching legs relax. But he hardly had time to recover before there was a great commotion of shouting and scuffling higher up the street. A truckload of German soldiers had arrived, and they were beginning to break up the groups of people. They were shouting orders and herding them into the main piazza at gunpoint. Paolo looked around desperately but he could see no means of escape, so was forced to mingle with the crowd, pushing his bicycle and hoping he wouldn't be noticed.

"What's happening?" he asked an old man who was jostling against him.

"The Partisans are coming out of hiding from the hills around here. Now that the *Inglesi* and the *Americani* are so near they want to fight out in the open. These Germans know they'll be pulling out of Florence soon and they're determined to kill as many Partisans as they can before they go. They hate them – especially the Reds. They hanged two of them the other day at Tuori. Now they've got our man."

"Il Volpe?"

"Yes – him. They know he comes from around here and they think we've been protecting him."

"What are they going to do to him?"

The old man merely spat on the ground and looked grimly ahead.

The little piazza was bordered on three sides by old houses, a police station and a few shops, all now closely shuttered. At one end was a fountain, enclosed by a low semi-circular wall, and at the other was an ancient archway, too narrow to accommodate modern vehicles. The church occupied the whole remaining side. Its façade was faced with striped green marble. There was a bell tower and two curved flights of steps leading up to the main doors. Below the steps was a crumbling wall covered with notices: orders to civilians from the occupying German army, and among them one or two fading images of Mussolini, the jutting-jawed dictator who had once been all-powerful but was now a failing puppet treated with contempt by the Nazis. The German soldiers were herding everyone into one half of the square, being careful to keep an empty space in front of the wall. There was an atmosphere of sullen resentment, but anyone who showed signs of disobedience was soon prodded into submission with the end of a rifle.

Paolo was pushed to the front of the crowd but somehow managed to hold on to his bicycle. He was weak with exhaustion and hunger now. The sweating strangers around him offered no reassurance. The crowd stood there, pressed together, waiting. At last, a squad of soldiers appeared leading Il Volpe. A couple of women cried out when they saw him, but most people remained silent. They all knew that they had been assembled to witness a public execution.

CHAPTER 20

"How could he have been such an idiot?" said Rosemary. "Going off like that with things as they are. Does he want to get himself killed?"

Constanza had just come in from searching the garden. Her dark eyes filled with fear when she heard that Paolo's bicycle was missing.

"He must have got some crazy idea into his head again about being a hero," she said. "Did he leave any kind of message?"

"Nothing. I was going to ring around the neighbours and ask if they've seen him – but I daren't draw too much attention to us. Not that we've many neighbours left. The Bonofantis and the Galleranis have already packed up. They've gone to take shelter in the Pensione Annalena before the fighting gets too near to the city. Those brave people who run it are offering shelter to anyone who needs it."

"Shouldn't we go too, Mamma?"

"We can't ... not with Joe still here and Paolo missing. We have to stay until Paolo turns up at least. I couldn't let him arrive home to find the place empty." She pressed both her hands tightly to her eyes. When she looked up at Constanza, it was with a carefully arranged expression of reassurance. "Don't worry, darling. We'll manage somehow. We'll just have to lie low here until Paolo gets back and it's safe for Joe to leave – tonight perhaps – and then we'll decide whether to join the others."

"Have Maria's brother and his family gone?"

"From the farm? No, they'll stay probably. Try to protect their property. The farm's all they have. But I don't care what happens to the house as long as you and Paolo are safe."

At that moment, there was a terrific explosion not far away which shook the ceiling. They could also hear sounds of turmoil coming from the kitchen. They hurried in to find Maria collapsed at the table in a storm of weeping, her head buried in her hands. Her brother Mario was sitting beside her, too distraught himself to offer any comfort.

"Whatever is it, Mario?" said Rosemary. "What's the matter? Is it Paolo? Has something happened to him?"

"No – no. It's my son Renato – my youngest. He's been arrested! The Gestapo have taken him."

"Arrested? But why?"

"They came early this morning and searched our house. They said we were suspected of helping Allied prisoners to escape. They turned everything upside down – wrecked our furniture and broke my wife's china. She got angry and tried to stop them. One of them pushed her, and she fell and hurt her arm. When Renato saw how they were treating her he tried to interfere, and he hit one of them. So they arrested him. They may have taken him into Florence to the Gestapo headquarters. God knows what they'll do to him there. I begged them not to take him. He's only just sixteen, not of military age yet. Just a boy…"

Rosemary was trying hard to think of something comforting to say.

"Don't worry too much yet," she managed in the end. "I'll see if we can make some enquiries as to where he's being held. It may be possible to make some plea on account of his age."

But Constanza, looking at her mother's white, shattered face, knew that exactly the same thought was going through both their minds, a question too terrifying to be asked aloud: what if this was what had happened to Paolo? It was a strong possibility.

They finally managed to calm Maria down, and her brother Mario hurried off to try and comfort his own family.

"He may have just gone off on one of his long bike rides," Constanza said to her mother when there was still no sign of him an hour later. "I bet he'll be back by lunchtime."

A mid-morning heat had settled over the house when one of Mario's daughters came running up to the back door, very excited. "Papà sent me," she said. "I'm to tell you that Renato's been released! They only kept him for a couple of hours and then they kicked him out."

"He's unharmed?" cried Maria.

"Yes, yes! He had to walk all the way back from Florence. He's sleeping now."

Tears of joy and relief ran down Maria's cheeks. "Oh, thank God, thank God! Renato is safe!"

Rosemary was on her feet at once to put her arms around her.

"Oh, Maria – I'm so glad," she managed to say. Inwardly, she was thinking, *Oh, Paolo, where are you? Why don't you come home?*

CHAPTER 21

The heat in the square was overwhelming. From where he was standing, Paolo could see the German soldiers push Il Volpe forward with their rifles. They shoved him up against the wall below the church doors, between the two flights of steps, and he stood there, sweating, sullen and clearly exhausted, but still upright. This was to be his place of execution.

The crowd was silent as the firing squad arrived, six more soldiers with an officer in charge. They formed a line with their backs to the crowd. It was customary, Paolo knew, to bandage the eyes of the condemned man before he was shot, but no one stepped forward to cover Il Volpe's eyes. He was clearly to be denied this mercy.

The whole square was deathly still now. The officer gave orders for the firing squad to raise their rifles. Paolo's stomach clenched and he thought he was going to be sick. He turned his face away and screwed up his eyes, waiting for the volley of fire.

It came, but not from the direction he had expected. He opened his eyes to see four men, armed with submachine-guns, burst out of the crypt very near to where Il Volpe was standing, firing as they ran. The red scarves over the lower half of their faces made their identity as Partisans unmistakable.

The execution squad were taken completely by surprise. One of them sprawled down, shot in the stomach, his blood spilling out onto the cobbles. The German officer was yelling orders at his men to regroup and return fire. One of the Partisans was hit in the leg but was dragged to safety by some men from the village.

And in that brief moment of confusion, Il Volpe saw his chance. He dodged behind his fellow Partisans and dived into the milling crowd. Paolo, who had been pushed forward in the panic, was now so close to him that they were face to face. For a split second they looked each other in the eye. Then, on a sudden impulse, Paolo thrust his bicycle towards Il Volpe, who grabbed it, mounted and pedalled off, dodging the gunfire as he careered towards the far side of the piazza. The crowd, clearly on his side, parted to allow his comrades to back after him, covering his escape.

People ducked as bullets ricocheted off walls. Women screamed. But Il Volpe had already disappeared, through the old gateway and down the narrow street where no vehicle could pursue him, like a fox gone to earth.

For those few vital minutes the Partisans had kept the soldiers at bay. Then they, too, disappeared after their leader. They had the advantage of knowing the warren of little streets that led away from the village far better than their pursuers. A German truck with a machine-gun entered the piazza, but its progress was blocked by people fleeing in all directions. Paolo ran with them, not knowing what else to do.

People were cramming into the side streets, running into their houses, pushing their children inside and slamming doors, trying to make themselves scarce while they had the chance. Paolo struggled back to the turning where he had entered the village.

He was so exhausted now that he could no longer think straight. Hunger and thirst were taking their toll on his strength. Worst of all, he no longer had his precious bicycle.

All he wanted now was to get away from this horrible place, these people and the inevitable brutal reprisals. As he left the village to begin the long trudge home, the sounds of battle sounded frighteningly close.

CHAPTER 22

They had only just begun to eat lunch when there was a knock at the front door. Constanza ran to answer it. Hilaria was standing on the doorstep. She was in a dishevelled state but still wearing her very high heels.

"Constanza! I've only got a minute but I couldn't go without saying goodbye! Mamma and Papà are waiting out on the road with the engine running. The car's loaded with stuff. They didn't want me to come here, but I made them stop. We're on our way north at last, to get away from the awful fighting. It'll be right here very soon, so it's our last chance. You're leaving too, I suppose?"

"Not for the moment."

"You don't mean you're staying here? It's so

dangerous! Everyone's leaving. The road into Florence is jammed. But listen" – her face was very flushed. Impulsively she reached out and took both of Constanza's hands – "I had to see you before we left. I had to tell you…"

"Tell me what?"

"It's…" She suddenly burst into tears. "It's about that day I dropped round to see you. A couple of days ago, remember? I thought there was something funny about the way you and Paolo were behaving, the way you didn't want me to go down into the cellar. As though you were hiding something."

"And?"

"Well…" Hilaria was clinging to her now. "Well … we heard afterwards that the Gestapo had been to search your house."

"Yes. And they found nothing, *nothing*!"

"I know… I know. But I just wanted to tell you that it wasn't me who tipped them off. I mean, we've always been friends, haven't we? Mamma and Papà didn't like it, what with your father's politics and all, but I never let that bother me, never!"

Constanza pushed Hilaria's hands away.

"*Don't* speak to me about my father," she said in

a very low voice. "My father has nothing to do with this, or with you."

Hilaria was becoming shrill with impatience.

"But you don't *understand*, Constanza! After they'd been to search your house I felt so awful. I mean, I may have let drop something about my suspicions to Aldo at some point. It was silly of me, I know. It just slipped out as a kind of joke when I was talking to him. He was – you know – leading me on to gossip about you and your family. He seemed sort of curious. But what I've come to tell you is that today I heard him talking to Colonel Richter on the phone. Aldo mentioned your mother's name, so I picked up the extension and I heard the colonel say her name was on some sort of list – a *Gestapo* list – of people who might be helping the Partisans. And that means she could be *shot*, Constanza! The colonel said he was sending soldiers back again to make another search. Really soon – today, probably. So you've just got to get away – all of you – right now!"

At that moment they heard a couple of urgent honks from the waiting car.

Hilaria hurriedly brushed away her tears and shook out her hair. "I've simply got to go. I'll see you again, I expect – when all this is over." She made an attempt to take Constanza's hands again but was met with a stony response.

"Goodbye, Hilaria."

"I'll send you a postcard with my new address. But I don't expect it'll arrive…"

"I said *goodbye*."

There was another honk on the horn. Hilaria hesitated uncertainly for a moment, then turned and ran off down the drive, unsteady on her high heels, waving over her shoulder but not looking back.

Constanza stood still in the doorway, her eyes tightly closed and her fists clenched. Then she ran inside to find her mother and warn Joe.

CHAPTER 23

"I'll be OK, honest," said Joe. He was scrambling into the workman's coat and cap he had worn for his previous escape. Rosemary was stuffing a bottle of water and what food they could spare into a shoulder bag.

"When you get to the main road, go in the opposite direction to Florence," she told him. "Most people will be trying to get to the north of the city to avoid the fighting. Just keep going until you come to one of the tracks that leads up into the hills. The Partisans are in control there."

"I'm coming with you," said Constanza. "Part of the way, at least."

Rosemary dropped the bag.

"Constanza – you *can't*! It's far too dangerous!"

"We'll be less likely to be noticed as a couple," said Constanza. "I can do all the talking if we're stopped. Then as soon as we're clear Joe can go on alone and make for the hills and I'll come straight back."

"No, Constanza. I won't let you, and that's final!"

"Your mom's right," said Joe. "I can manage fine on my own and once I've contacted the Partisans they'll help me."

But he looked pale and shaky, hardly fit for a long walk in the punishing heat, let alone another possible encounter with German soldiers on the way.

Constanza had a look on her face that her mother knew well, one which since childhood had signalled a steely determination to accomplish exactly what she had made up her mind to do – it nearly always resulted in her getting her own way. She was already taking Maria's shawl from the peg and pulling it around her shoulders.

"We'll need some money," she said. "And—" But she was cut short by the sound of wheels on the gravel outside the front door and a voice shouting orders in German. It seemed that the search party had arrived even earlier than expected. Rosemary ran into the hall. This time there was no polite ring at the doorbell and no Colonel Richter or Lieutenant Gräss to engage in conversation. The door was simply flung open and a German Army sergeant burst in, followed by four private soldiers with rifles at the ready.

Rosemary confronted them as bravely as she could.

"What do you want?" she asked in German.

The sergeant was a man in his early thirties, well built but already running to fat. He had the weary, short-tempered look of a professional soldier who had not had any leave for a very long time.

"Have you a warrant to come in here?" she asked him, coolly polite. "A very thorough search of this house has already been made, you know."

"We're under orders from the Gestapo to make a further search. There's been another report made to headquarters that you may be hiding Allied servicemen, enemies of the Reich, here, and aiding their escape."

"There's nobody here but myself, my children and my maid, Maria."

The sergeant didn't answer but motioned briskly

with his rifle for two of his men to start their search upstairs. Then, followed by the other two, he pushed past her and hurried down the passage that led to the kitchen.

We're finished, thought Rosemary, with a great pang of desperation. *This is the end of everything.* She felt sick with fear.

Maria emerged from the kitchen, complaining shrilly and attempting to bar their way, but she was soon thrust aside. They pushed open the door – and found Constanza sitting alone at the long wooden table with a plate of grapes and some bread in front of her. She looked up as they came in with a fawn-like expression of innocent alarm that would have melted the heart of the most battle-weary soldier. The sergeant muttered something at her as the soldiers began their search of the room, the pantries and the washhouse. Rosemary caught her breath with relief when she noticed that the door to the yard was ajar. Constanza must have got Joe out of the way just in time.

Upstairs, the other soldiers were going through the house from top to bottom. This time they made no attempt to restore the chaos they were leaving behind them. They were extremely thorough. They paid particular attention when they reached the cellar.

Rosemary and Constanza went to the top of the stairs and watched, huddled together, as they ransacked their way through it, shining torches into every corner. All the junk that had been carefully put back in front of Joe's hiding place was pulled away and the poor old uniformed dummy toppled. There was a cry of triumph when they found the little door to the wine store. The soldiers took aim with their rifles as the sergeant flung it open. There was an awkward pause when they found it empty. One of the men swore under his breath but was barked into silence by the sergeant.

"There's nobody here, as you see," said Rosemary in loud clear German. "Colonel Richter's party was here before, as you know, and found nothing, because there's nothing to find. I'm afraid you're wasting your time. But perhaps you would like to make a further search of the garden and outhouses? I want it on record that we have been absolutely co-operative."

She caught Constanza's eye with a glance that said "Where is he?" but there was no flicker of response. The two women stood aside as the search party trooped back up the cellar stairs. The sergeant was angry and still suspicious. Without another word to Rosemary, he ordered his men outside and then stamped out after them. They heard him shouting orders as the soldiers fanned out across the dried-up garden, beating bushes and trampling over what used to be Rosemary's flowerbeds, working their way towards the outhouses and the yard. Rosemary and Constanza waited inside. Rosemary took Constanza's hand. It trembled in hers as they both stood there, listening, hardly able to move.

They could hear Guido's frantic barking from the yard. Then there were shots, and Constanza's brave reserve broke down. She clung to her mother, burying her face in her shoulder.

There was a long, terrible silence, then a lot of shouting. At last the sergeant reappeared at the front door. He ordered his men to bring the truck round. The soldiers climbed in. When they were all on board the sergeant slung his rifle over his shoulder and turned to the two women. His face was expressionless. "*Heil* Hitler," he said, then saluted, jumped into the truck beside the driver and gave orders to move on.

Rosemary was very pale. Slowly, as though her feet were weighted down, she went to the door and looked after them.

"He was in the yard," whispered Constanza, then covered her face with her hands.

"You'd better stay here, darling. I'll go and see what's happened," Rosemary said. But as she made her way round to the yard she could hear Constanza following behind her. She was terrified of what they might find.

"Don't come – don't. Stay inside," she insisted. "It would be much better, really. Please."

But Constanza took no notice.

The yard was weirdly silent. And there, lying stretched out on the ground as far away from his kennel as his lead would allow, lay Guido's dead body. He had been shot three times in the head. The flies were already beginning to collect in the jagged hole where his eyes had once been and on the sticky mess of blood and brains that were seeping from it onto the ground beneath. Constanza made a kind of strangled cry. She stood stock-still beside Rosemary for a moment, then she knelt down and very gently touched his blood-soaked fur.

"Guido," she said in a very low voice. She turned to the kennel. There was a movement inside and Joe crawled out from the dark interior. He squatted down beside her and put his good arm around her shoulders.

"Poor old Guido," he said. "He knew he was protecting me and he put up a great fight. He barked and snarled and pulled on his chain until it nearly choked him. So one of those swine put three bullets into him. And not one of them thought of looking inside the kennel."

Tears had begun to course down Constanza's cheeks. She was too distraught to wipe them away.

"It was the only place I could think of for you to hide," she said.

"He saved my life," said Joe. "You and Guido both."

CHAPTER 24

With Maria's help, Constanza and Rosemary wrapped Guido's body in a sheet and dragged him out of the yard to one of the outhouses, where it was cool and quiet.

"We'll have to bury him quickly," said Rosemary. "If only Paolo…" Then she stopped short. The thought of Paolo's reaction to Guido's death, on top of everything else, was almost more than she could bear.

Maria was unexpectedly calm in the face of death. She stopped her customary flood of scolding and complaints, led Rosemary into the kitchen and sat her down at the table. While she was looking in the cupboard to see if there was any coffee left,

Rosemary suddenly slumped sideways on her chair, covering her eyes with her hand.

"I'm sorry, Maria – I seem to be feeling faint… Could you…?"

Maria caught her as she fell.

When she came round she was lying on the drawing-room sofa with Maria bending over her.

"I'm all right, really," she said, attempting to prop herself up on her elbow. "It was silly of me…"

"*Rimanga qui, signora!* Stay there a little. You've had too much for anyone to take today."

"If I could have a glass of water?"

"Surely, surely. I'll get it. Stay there and rest."

"But I can't. I mustn't. If only Paolo would come home. He really ought to be back by now. And Constanza and Joe – where are they?"

"Not in the house. In the yard, perhaps. I'll get them for you."

She hurried away. But the yard, house and garden were silent and empty. Constanza and Joe had already set out, hand in hand, and were on the road, making their way among the steadily building stream of people who were fleeing from the fighting.

*   *   *

The late-afternoon sun was suffocatingly hot. The road was clogged with cyclists, families pushing handcarts that groaned under the weight of their belongings, and nuns shepherding groups of children. Motorists were honking their horns and trying to edge forward through the crowd. Weary Italian soldiers, some wounded, were trudging north in an attempt to rejoin their units. Everyone was too intent on their own survival to pay much attention to anyone else. The sound of shellfire was alarmingly near now, sometimes spasmodic, sometimes a sustained barrage that shook the ground under their feet. A convoy of army trucks packed with soldiers suddenly rounded the bend, followed by a couple of machine-gun carriers, and everyone scattered as they forced their way through. Joe put his good arm protectively around Constanza.

"I shouldn't have let you do this," he said.

"But I wanted to," she insisted.

"And I wanted it too. But it was selfish of me, I guess. I just couldn't say goodbye to you in the yard after what happened, and all you've done for me."

Constanza said nothing. She just shook her head and smiled. They walked on in silence, keeping up a steady pace until they reached the turning where the track led off into the hills. Here, Joe stopped and said, "I'm not letting you come any further. This is where we have to say goodbye."

"Is your shoulder OK?"

"Yeah, it'll be fine."

"The Partisans are coming out of hiding now. They're very strong in this area, and the local people won't bother you. Just make sure they know you are Canadian."

"I'll let you know where I fetch up if – I mean, *when* I get through. I'll write you. I'm not much good at letters, but—"

"I am. I'll write back. It'll be good for my English!"

"I'm no good at saying how I feel. It all turns out like a lot of garbage from some B movie. Especially when I look at you, your eyes, and the way you push your hair back over your ears like that, like a kid. How old are you, anyway?"

"Nearly seventeen."

"I'm so much older than you."

"How old?"

"Twenty-one. But fighting a war's an ageing business, I guess. You have to shut down such a lot of yourself, just concentrate on staying alive. In the camp, the only thing that keeps you going is the dream of what you'll do when you get out – imagining someone like you…"

"I hate this war. I hate you and me and my family having to be in it. I hate hardly being able to remember what things were like before it all began. Oh, Joe, do you think we'll ever be able to go dancing?"

"Sure. Sure we will."

"I'll think about it. I'll imagine the dress I'll wear."

"And I'll imagine you wearing it."

"Now you've got to go."

"Yeah. I've got to go."

He put both his arms around her and, ignoring his poor shoulder, they clung together with a kind of fierce desperation. It was an awkward embrace, but the kiss that followed was the world-shaking kind, the kind that goes down in history, the kind you always remember. When Joe had gone a little way up the road he turned to wave to her but she was already walking away, very fast. She didn't turn around.

Constanza managed to walk some distance from the spot where she had left Joe before she began to cry.

She kept on walking, half blinded by tears and wiping them away with the palms of her hands because she had no handkerchief. She was thinking about Joe kissing her, and the possibility that she might never see him again, and then about the horror of Guido's death, still so raw in her mind, and about the whole frightening mess that she and her family were in, and there being nothing, *nothing* to look forward to now except the end of this horrible war, and heaven knew when that would be.

Up until then she had always thought of the day she had said goodbye to Babbo – not then fully understanding why he had to leave them – as the blackest in her life. But that seemed like a long time ago, when she had still been almost a child. She felt far older now and everything had got far, far worse.

When she reached the main road, she found it more crowded than ever. She tried to jostle through but nobody was in the mood to give way and she only just managed to avoid being pushed into the ditch by a man and his wife leading a horse and cart piled high with assorted furniture, a pen full of live chickens, some cooking pots and a large mattress with two children and a dog perched on top. Constanza stopped for a moment, exhausted, her tears still coming as though there were no end to them. Then she heard someone call her name. For a moment she thought Joe had come back to find her, and her heart leapt with joy. Then she realized that it was an even more familiar voice.

"Paolo!" she shouted back.

She could see his head bobbing along some way off. He was waving.

"Oh, Paolo – thank God!"

They struggled towards each other. Paolo looked every bit as exhausted as she was, and he was clearly so close to tears that she stopped crying and hugged him.

"Paolo – where have you been all this time? Where's your bicycle?"

"I lost it. I mean, I gave it to someone."

"Gave it? What on earth…? But let's get out of this crowd and you can tell me about it. This road's hopeless. I think we should go round the other way, take the back road and cut across to the farm. We've got to hurry. Mamma'll be worried sick."

This was clearly not the time to tell him all that had happened at home that day, and especially not about

Guido. As they doubled back, Paolo began to pour out a rather incoherent account of his own exploits, but when he tried to explain what had happened to his bicycle he could not go on. He fell silent and Constanza didn't press him. They kept walking by sheer effort of will, their legs sore and tired; one strap on Constanza's flimsy sandal had broken and Paolo was hardly able to put one foot after another. When they reached the side road they found it unusually deserted.

"It's a longer walk but it'll take us less time now we're clear of all those people," said Constanza. Paolo was too weary to answer. Suddenly, out of nowhere, two aircraft ripped through the sky overhead, and there was a series of ear-splitting explosions as three bombs hit the hillside just across the valley. A barn caught fire and heavy smoke began to drift towards them. Instinctively, they covered their heads with their hands.

"Allied planes," said Paolo, "harassing the German retreat. Those planes are trying to knock out their gun emplacements."

"Come on, Paolo – let's try to go faster," urged Constanza. "I can't bear to think of Mamma being alone at home with only Maria."

She quickened her pace and Paolo stumbled

along behind her. They could hear the noise of heavy gunfire, frighteningly near. Then there was the sound of vehicles coming up the road behind them. A truckload of German soldiers bumped into view, followed by an armoured car with an officer and a sergeant on board. Paolo and Constanza drew back into the hedge to let them pass but they pulled up a few feet away. The officer jumped out of the car and strode towards them.

"Helmut!" breathed Constanza. Paolo said nothing. They had both reached the point where they were beyond surprise.

CHAPTER 25

Helmut's appearance was no longer that of the smartly turned out young German officer. His uniform was covered with dust and sweat and his face drawn with exhaustion. He shouted an order over his shoulder and the truck driver turned off his engine. "What are you doing here?" Lieutenant Helmut Gräss asked angrily. "Do you realize how dangerous it is to be out here on this road? The enemy are advancing very near here."

"I – we…" began Constanza and then stopped. It was all just too difficult to explain. "I came to meet Paolo," she continued lamely. "He's been – he had an accident and lost his bicycle."

"You must turn back at once," Helmut said

impatiently. "This road isn't safe. The Partisans have planted mines everywhere. You must get back to the main road."

"But we've got to get home quickly. We're worried about my mother being on her own."

"You should never have come out here."

"You are retreating?"

"Yes – yes, we are retreating. My men have had no sleep for two nights now. The bridges over the Arno are being blown up, all but the Ponte Vecchio, which is blocked at both ends. General Schlemm is occupying the north of the city and we need to make a detour to regroup further up the river. So, as you see, this is no time for polite conversation."

"Of course we'll turn back if you say we must. Right away. But Helmut" – she impulsively put out her hand to him – "before we go, I just want to say… I mean, I hope you get through this all right."

This sounded ridiculously lame and schoolgirlish, she thought, but she meant it with all her heart. It came from the real affection she felt for him and the huge gratitude for the day when he had led the search party at their house and somehow managed not to notice that scrap of incriminating evidence on the floor of their cellar. She knew he had done it out of friendship, for her sake and for her family, and that it had gone against all his disciplined instincts as a German officer. Her feelings for him had nothing to do with the hatred she felt for the side he was fighting for. Sides didn't seem very relevant at that particular moment.

He hesitated, then took her hand and held it. For a minute all the anger left his face. He looked at her intently as though he was trying to store something vitally important in his memory. Then he pulled away, saluted and turned back to his men.

He ordered the truck to stay where it was. His sergeant jumped down then and brought out a mine detector. Paolo, who had been watching the scene from where he was resting his weary feet on the bank, guessed what was about to happen. Helmut and his sergeant were going to go on ahead to test the next stretch of road for mines. The Partisans tended to plant them at the sides of the road rather than in the middle, but that was by no means certain and even with a detector, this was a dangerous operation. If the road was clear the truck would follow.

The two men disappeared around the bend in the

lane. A tense silence descended, broken only by the buzzing of cicadas. The shellfire across the valley seemed to have ceased. The men on the truck sat immobile, listening. The minutes dragged by slowly. Constanza clutched Paolo's arm. They were all concentrating on the moment when those two men would reappear; each person was willing them to walk back around the bend.

Suddenly the silence was broken by an ear-splitting roar as an explosion tore through the air. There was a blast of heat as though from an oven, and flame, earth and foliage shot upwards. Immediately several men jumped down from the truck and ran around the bend in the road. Constanza and Paolo tried to follow them but one of the soldiers ordered them to stay back. All they could do was stand and wait.

Everything seemed to go into slow motion. At last the soldiers reappeared. Two of them were supporting the sergeant. His face was badly cut and streaming with blood. The others were carrying Helmut, his arms trailing, his body hanging limp between them. They laid him on the bank, near to where Constanza and Paolo were standing, and covered him with their jackets. He lay perfectly still. Ignoring all warnings to keep back, Constanza knelt beside him. His face and shoulders were amazingly unharmed, but she could not bear to look at the rest of him. He was muttering, trying to say something. He put out a hand towards her and she took it. She tried to find the right reassuring words in German but found that they utterly failed her. All she could do was to stroke his hand very gently and say, "Helmut … Helmut … it's all right, Helmut." She thought she heard him say something that sounded like "My mother … tell my mother…" He closed his eyes, then opened them again and seemed for a moment to recognize her. Meanwhile, one of the men ran to fetch a first-aid kit from the car and another put a rolled-up shirt under Helmut's head.

"We'll get help," she told him desperately. Blood was soaking copiously through the jacket that covered his legs and was spilling out onto the grass. One of his men was attempting to staunch the flow by tying a scarf tightly above what was left of his right knee. Another was trying to assist his breathing. Constanza felt useless and started to move out of the way, but he held onto her hand. He was trying to speak again and she lowered her ear very close to his mouth, straining to catch the words, but they were garbled and unintelligible. She knew that it was only a matter of minutes before the trauma of the explosion gave way to the agony of his injuries and he would start to scream. Somebody put a water bottle to his lips, but he was unable to drink.

Then his face changed. He was no longer looking at her. He seemed focused on something further away, something he couldn't see clearly. Suddenly, he wasn't looking at anything at all. His hand went limp in hers. She murmured his name again, very softly. But he didn't hear her. It was as though something invisible had escaped, light as a feather, from his open mouth. It took her some minutes before she realized he was dead.

CHAPTER 26

A few miles away Joe was still walking. He was fairly deep into the countryside now and the brisk pace he had attempted at the start of his journey was slowing down. He was sweating heavily and his shoulder wound was throbbing badly. From time to time he encountered local people on the track carrying their children and pathetically few belongings, but they were far too desperate to get away from the tide of war to take any notice of him. So far he had seen no Partisans. He had hoped to meet up with them by now. He knew they were operating openly all over this area now, harassing the retreating Germans and taking summary revenge on local Fascists. But where were they? Not in this particular area, it seemed.

The sun was going down. Joe began to wonder anxiously if he had taken the wrong road or missed a turning. His head was aching so much that he began to doubt his sense of direction. Some RAF planes flew overhead and he looked up at them with grim satisfaction. It seemed like the battle for Florence was in its last stages. But here on the ground he was far from safe. If he met up with any Germans he would probably be shot right here on this track. One thing was sure: he was too tired to run.

He sat down for a brief rest, grateful for the flask of water and small pack of food Rosemary had given him. The temptation to stretch out on the grass and fall asleep was enormous, but he knew he had to keep going. Constanza's face when they had said goodbye kept coming back to him. *What a heck of a sweet kid.* He wished he had been able to find the words to tell her how he felt about her; her bravery, the way she held her head, her eyes – all the things he so desperately wanted to remember about her. He was well aware that being locked up all that time in the prison camp might have made him overly susceptible to the first good-looking girl he met, but he was convinced she was special. Back in the camp, he had envied David, who had a special girl waiting for him in England, and the joy her letters gave him when those longed-for Red Cross deliveries came through. There had been girls in his own life, of course. There were always plenty of women around wherever there were army camps. But never anyone who would bother to write to him. He wondered where David was now. Back behind the wire maybe, poor guy – if he was alive at all. Joe knew he shouldn't be thinking about all this now. With a great effort, he heaved himself to his feet and tried to concentrate his mind and what was left of his energy on his own immediate survival. The artillery barrage seemed to be coming from the area just to the north of where he was, a constant exchange of fire. He had a nasty feeling that this plan of escape was going horribly wrong.

He had hardly begun to walk on before there came the sudden sound of an approaching vehicle. It was on him before he had time to hide. All he could do was to stop stock-still in the middle of the track and face whatever was coming. A tank came rumbling around the bend and he found himself staring into the muzzle of a gun pointing straight at him. *This is it,* he thought. *This is the end.* He held his hands up over his head and shouted, "Don't shoot! I'm unarmed!"

There was a short pause. Then a head appeared and a voice called out in English, "Who are you?"

"I'm Sergeant Joe Zolinski of the First Canadian Division. I'm an escaped prisoner of war and I demand full rights under the Geneva Convention."

"Hey! What the hell are you doing here?" came the answer. Slowly, it dawned on Joe that this was not a German speaking in English. It was a real Canadian accent, one he hadn't heard for far too long. He took another look at the tank and realized with a sudden burst of almost unbearable joy and relief that it was not a German one but a "Grizzly" – a Canadian M4.

A soldier in Canadian uniform jumped out and walked over to him, accompanied by another, who kept him covered with a rifle, just in case. Joe kept his arms aloft but his face broke into a huge grin. "Boy, am I glad to see you!" he said.

"We're with the First Canadian Armoured Brigade. We're moving north. Won't be long before we've got Gerry licked this side of the Arno, at least. Hop on board. We'll give you a lift."

CHAPTER 27

It was almost midnight when Constanza and Paolo trudged up the drive. Rosemary ran out to meet them. She threw her arms around both of them, too overwhelmed with relief to say very much. All the questions could wait. The eternity she seemed to have spent praying for their safe arrival was over, and that was all that mattered.

Maria conjured up some hot water for a bath and put out something to eat. Paolo tucked in ravenously but Constanza hardly touched what was on her plate. They were both very quiet, clearly too exhausted to relate the events of their day. Rosemary knew better than to press them now. "Thank God you're back," she kept saying. "Thank God."

The moment she most dreaded came when they had finished eating and she realized that she had to break it to Paolo that Guido was dead. He broke down completely when she told him, covering his face with his hands and sobbing uncontrollably.

"How *could* they?" he kept repeating. "Poor, poor Guido!"

"He was always a brave dog," Rosemary said. "And he died saving Joe's life."

"Those Nazi swine! I'd like to shoot *them*. Guido's been my dog since I was nine. He was my friend! I just can't imagine being without him."

There was nothing anyone could say that would console him. He wanted to run out to Guido there and then, but Rosemary had to explain that she and Maria had already buried him with the help of Maria's nephew Renato.

"We had to do it," she said quietly. "It was entirely necessary in this heat. We've made a grave for him in the garden under the big cypress tree. When you've had some sleep you can think about making something to mark the place."

"How can I sleep now?" Paolo almost screamed. "How can I, after what's happened to me today?"

And he rushed out into the dark to find the spot where Guido was buried.

Rosemary turned desperately to Constanza. "I couldn't let Paolo see Guido in the state he was in," she said. "I wanted at least to spare him that."

Constanza said nothing, but Rosemary saw that tears were coursing down her cheeks. She put an arm around her.

"We all need some sleep," she said.

But sleep was almost impossible that night. The Germans had moved their batteries even nearer and the Crivellis could hear great thudding explosions so close that it seemed the roof might fall in at any moment. And the electricity had been cut off.

Rosemary wondered if they should all shelter in the cellar but in the end settled for piling some cushions on the drawing-room floor. It was well after one in the morning before Paolo at last reappeared, tear-stained and distraught. They huddled under blankets on the makeshift mattresses – all except Maria, who had refused to leave the comfort of her own bed.

Somewhere in the early hours Paolo and

Constanza finally fell asleep, poleaxed with exhaustion. Rosemary lay wedged between them, staring into the dark. She was thinking about Franco. It was almost unbearable not to have him here with them now, and even worse to have no news of him. She wondered if Paolo and Constanza were forgetting him. They hardly ever mentioned him, which was not surprising, considering all they were going through. But right now they needed him more than ever, and so did she. And when he did come back, she wondered, what then? If they survived this war would he expect them all to settle down to tranquil family life again? They were different people now. He had left behind two much-loved children and he would return to a couple of young adults who had been forced to experience things from which no one, not even she, had been able to protect them.

As if to reinforce her fears there was a particularly huge explosion. It shook the ceiling, and bits of plaster fell onto their makeshift bed. *We should have gone into the cellar,* she thought grimly. But she didn't have the heart to wake the two oblivious sleepers beside her.

Lying there, tensely bracing herself for the

next explosion, she found herself thinking about her mother. The Germans had boasted about their terrifying new weapons – pilotless rocket planes – with which they had attacked London and south-east England. And, with the noise of bombardment ringing in her own ears, Rosemary wondered if she would ever see her mother again.

The early dawn was just breaking when Rosemary heard Maria's angry voice raised outside. A moment later, she came hurrying in still wearing her dressing-gown and her formidable helmet-like hairnet.

"Come quickly, *signora*!" she cried. "There are German soldiers in the yard demanding food! Some of them are even washing at the pump – nearly naked except for their underpants! *Che vergogna!*"

Rosemary struggled to her feet, careful not to wake her children. Soldiers, naked or otherwise, were the last thing she wanted to contend with at this hour, but she hurried with Maria into the yard.

The men there looked terribly demoralized, more like a rabble than a platoon of well-disciplined German infantry. Many of them had leant their weapons against the wall while they doused themselves under the tap; others were slumped about on the ground, utterly exhausted. Rosemary glanced around for the officer in charge. At last he appeared, looking almost as dishevelled as his men, and ordered them to dress themselves and form up. He gave her a perfunctory "*Heil* Hitler!" salute but she noticed that his hand returned quite quickly to his revolver. He was a hard-eyed young man somewhere in his mid twenties.

"Good morning," she said politely in German. She was thinking fast, in spite of her weariness. There had been local stories of looting, of houses ransacked, and not only for food and money but for all kinds of things such as waterproofs, jewellery, watches, live fowl and even sunglasses. There had been darker tales of violence, too. She thought of Constanza still lying peacefully asleep on the drawing-room floor and her heart turned over with fear, but she faced the officer as bravely as she could.

"We have hardly any food left," she said. "But we do have some barley bread and fruit."

He nodded.

"We'll bring it out for you." As she and Maria hurried into the kitchen, she whispered, "*Whatever happens, we mustn't let them into the house!"*

The men ate ravenously and washed the food down with great gulps of water from the tap. The officer's mood seemed slightly improved after he had eaten. He eyed the back door.

"You are alone here, *signora*?"

"This is our family home. My husband will be back any moment now."

"And the rest of the family?"

"Inside."

"You have children?"

"Yes. I told you. They are inside."

There was a tinge of insolence in his look now.

"Your German is very good."

"Thank you."

He paused. She could see him trying to peer in through one of the windows. She was too frightened to speak.

"We need—" he began. But he was cut off in mid-sentence by a shattering explosion so near that for a moment Rosemary thought the house had received a direct hit. Smoke drifted across the yard from the garden. A shell must have landed there, missing them all by only a few hundred yards.

"We seem to be very near the front line," she said shakily.

He looked at her, half contemptuous, and she thought she had never seen so much world-weariness in such a young face.

"*Signora*, you are *on* the front line," he said.

Then he turned to his men and barked out a few orders. They straightened up and shouldered their rifles. She and Maria watched them trudge out of the yard in ragged formation. There could be few more depressing sights, she thought, than soldiers in retreat, wondering where they would be by nightfall, or even if they would be alive at all.

CHAPTER 28

All that day the bombardment continued. In the end it was so bad that they all went down to shelter in the cellar, taking what food they had left. They had an electric torch and there was a little oil left in the lamps but they decided to save them for an emergency and huddled together in the darkness. Paolo and Constanza dozed fitfully; Maria alternated between praying and complaining under her breath. The old dummy in its elaborate uniform loomed from the shadows, juddering with every fresh explosion but still managing to remain upright. The hours dragged by. Rosemary was amazed when she looked at her watch and found that it was only four o'clock in the afternoon.

At last she drifted into sleep. She had no idea how

long she had slept when she was suddenly jerked awake by the sound of someone moving about in the yard.

"Hello?" It was a man's voice, unmistakably speaking in English. "Hello? Is there anyone there?"

She jumped up, panic-stricken. Leaving the others still sleeping, she ran upstairs to the kitchen, flung open the back door and called out, "Who are you? What do you want?"

It was dark outside. A figure in uniform stepped forward and saluted briskly.

"Ah, you speak English! Splendid!" he said, and held out his hand. "Captain Roberts. I'm a signals officer attached to the Sixth South African Armoured Division. Terribly sorry if I frightened you. I just wasn't sure if this place was empty or not."

"I am *Signora* Crivelli, and I am English. This is my home. Are you an escaped prisoner?"

"Oh, no, no! Not at all. Quite the reverse. Didn't you know? Since noon today this area has been in Allied hands. We're already in Florence, occupying the south of the city. I'm afraid I've come to ask you to accommodate my men here in your grounds and around the house. We'll need to set up a communications centre here, rooms for my wireless operators and so forth. We'll try not to be too much of a nuisance."

A nuisance! Rosemary's first impulse was to fling her arms around him and welcome him with tears of joy but she managed to restrain herself. Instead, she held the door open wide and said, "Delighted to see you, Captain Roberts. Do come in!"

Early the next morning Paolo emerged into the sunlight to find the drive full of army vehicles and soldiers all over the garden putting up tents. The whole place was such a hive of activity that it helped take his mind off the sadness of Guido's death. He wandered around, watching the work and trying out his English.

It took some time for the wonderful reality of the situation to sink in: the Nazi occupation was over. The battle for Florence had been fought bloodily, street by street, by Partisans and trained soldiers alike. The sound of artillery fire was still clearly audible in the hills surrounding the city and there was a lot of aircraft activity overhead. But the scent of victory was in the air and now, perhaps, that hated swastika would be gone from the Piazza Del Publico for ever.

Avoiding the spot were Guido was buried, Paolo went to look at the big torn-up crater in the vegetable garden where the shell had landed the day before. It had been a very near thing. It could have so easily been a direct hit.

At last, realizing that he was achingly hungry, he went into the kitchen, where he found Maria in excellent high spirits, stowing away food.

"Look at this, Paolo! Look at what the soldiers have given us! Flour, ham, olive oil, cheese and coffee, as well as all this canned stuff! *Che meraviglia!*" Joyfully she held up a tin of corned beef. "We've got some milk too. I managed to get across to the farm early this morning. Sit down and have some breakfast. Your mamma and Constanza are still asleep."

After he had eaten, Paolo went to watch Captain Roberts and his team at work. They had completely cleared the dining room and were busy setting up their wireless equipment. He longed to ask all kinds of questions about how it operated but he was too shy to bother them. Instead, he hung about in the background, trying to keep out of their way, thrilled to be looking on at the purposeful Captain Roberts's world and, even better, knowing that they were Allied soldiers who were not to be feared. The memories of that sun-baked village square, the packed, sweating crowd awaiting that summary execution still haunted him. They kept running and re-running in his head, a sequence of sinister, surreal images which wouldn't go away. He wondered what had happened to Il Volpe and his fellow Partisans. Had they managed to escape or had they been shot, or hanged from lamp-posts, like so many of their comrades? More selfishly, he also wondered what had happened to his bicycle.

The whole family were drinking coffee in the kitchen – *coffee*, the first proper cup they had tasted for a long time – when they heard the sound of cheering coming from the road. Constanza and Paolo ran out to see what was happening. All the local people who had not evacuated to a safer zone were outside. There was great excitement.

"Is it the Canadians?" asked Constanza, full of hope, and thinking of Joe.

"No, no! The Partisans! They're out in the open, showing themselves at last – heading towards the city!"

Constanza and Paolo craned their necks as the procession came into view riding in trucks, open cars and armoured personnel carriers. It was a ragged army, wearing patched trousers, shabby caps, berets and sweat-stained shirts, with ammunition belts slung around their shoulders. Able at last to proudly display their red bandanas, they waved their rifles and fired bullets into the air to acknowledge the cheering. Women handed them flowers. Girls kissed them. Then the cry went up: "Il Volpe! Il Volpe!" And there he was on the open truck – bare-head, haggard face, foxy eyes, red beard and all – surrounded by his henchmen and triumphantly acknowledging his rightful acclaim.

Paolo cheered himself hoarse with the rest. He had not quite forgotten that menacing encounter in the hills – the punch in the stomach, the guns prodding him in the back. But that seemed like another era, a time when he had been so much more innocent about the brutalities of war. He knew about them now, all right. It wasn't a simple matter of the good guys and the bad guys, that was certain. But, still, he cheered.

The crowd surged towards the truck on which Il Volpe was riding, slowing it down. Everyone was reaching up their hands to shake his and yelling, *"Viva, viva! Viva* Il Volpe!"

It was only a short hold-up. But in that brief moment Il Volpe spotted Paolo. And, as in their desperate confrontation in the piazza, when death had come so close, they looked each other straight in the eye over the sea of heads. Il Volpe raised his hand in a salute and called out something, but Paolo couldn't catch the words. Then the truck moved on, making its way in triumph towards Florence.

Paolo and Constanza walked home in silence, both too dazed to talk. But Paolo felt a new comradeship between them, maybe something to do with her acceptance of him as a fellow adult instead of a kid brother. And he guessed that a great deal had happened to her recently that was very private to her and not to be shared with anyone. When they reached the house she went straight to her room and he heard the familiar sound of her gramophone.

He wandered off towards the yard. The pain of seeing Guido's empty kennel had to be faced, and he wanted to make sure that the soldiers hadn't moved it. Another dog might live in it one day but there would never, ever, be one as faithful, brave and as such a true friend as Guido. Paolo was already planning to use Babbo's woodcarving tools to carve a really beautiful panel for the grave. Perhaps when the war was over they would even have a marble headstone. On his way to the yard he passed the bicycle shed. He walked on, then stopped dead in his tracks. He retraced his steps and again stood still in amazement. There, propped up against Maria's old boneshaker, was his beloved bicycle!

He pulled it out and looked at it. It had been cleaned. He clasped the handlebars as though it was some wonderful mirage that might suddenly disappear. He tried the brakes and found they were working beautifully. Then he noticed a sheet of roughly torn paper pushed under the saddle. He unfolded it and read: RETURNED WITH THANKS. There was no signature. A British Army corporal passed by carrying a pile of boxes. He stopped and said casually, "Your bike, is it?"

"Yes … yes. I thought I'd lost it."

"Valuable things, bikes, these days."

"Do you know how it got here?"

"Oh yes – didn't anyone tell you? Some Italians brought it here very early this morning – before dawn, it was. Didn't speak any English and the sentry who stopped them doesn't speak a word of their lingo. But they managed to explain that they were returning the bike."

"What sort of men were they?"

"Partisans, by the look of them. Rifles, red scarves around their necks and that. They're all over the place around here now."

"Was one of them a ginger-haired guy with a beard?"

The man shrugged. "Can't say. I wasn't around at the time. You can ask the sentry when he comes back on watch again."

"Thanks. I will."

"You've got your bike back, anyway. That's the main thing, isn't it?"

"Yes," said Paolo happily. "Yes, it certainly is."

CHAPTER 29

Rosemary was walking to church in the evening sunshine. A night's sleep in her own bed had done wonders for her morale. There had been an important Mass that Sunday morning for the entire village, which she had attended with Constanza and Paolo, but now she was going alone to say her own private prayers. She was full of gratitude, relieved beyond words that her two children were safe. What did she care now that soldiers were all over her house creating chaos, encamped in what had once been her garden, pitching their tents and setting up field kitchens, shouting orders, installing their equipment and, from time to time, stretching out wearily on the grass? The house was still standing and Constanza and Paolo were alive, and right now that was all that mattered. She felt a strong need to give thanks. She might lack her mother's rock-solid faith – her father's and Franco's scepticism were still a powerful influence on her – but even so she clung to her church.

It was a quiet, thinly attended Mass. Maria's brother Mario and his wife were there with their two daughters and their youngest son, Renato. Prayers were said for the Archbishop of Florence, Cardinal Dalla Costa, who had stood out so courageously against the Nazis during the occupation, offering to take the place of some of his nuns when they were arrested for harbouring Jewish women. There were a few Allied servicemen in the congregation as well, and afterwards they stood outside in the sunshine, exchanging greetings with the local people just as the German officers had done such a little time ago.

Rosemary was on her way home when she realized that Mario was following close behind her. He was alone. His family had gone in the opposite direction, back to the farm to make the supper. When she turned to greet him she saw that he was terribly troubled and there were tears in his eyes.

"Mario, is everything all right?"

"*Signora* Crivelli – please – I need to speak to you."

"Of course. Won't you come back to the house? It's rather chaotic up there, as you know, but we could find a quiet place somewhere, I'm sure."

"No, no. I'd rather not. I must say what I have to right here."

"Tell me what's wrong, Mario. You're not in trouble?"

Mario's face crumpled and he began to weep.

"I have something to tell you, something I have already confessed to the priest," he said. "It's about that time when Renato was arrested by the Gestapo … that terrible day when they took him to their interrogation headquarters in Florence."

"Of course, I remember it only too well. And how relieved we all were when he was released."

"But it was not quite as you think. Not at all. They threatened Renato with torture, you see. A boy not yet seventeen! They told us beforehand what they were going to do to him if we didn't co-operate."

"Co-operate? How do you mean?"

"This is what I have to tell you. They already suspected very strongly that you and your children were helping Allied prisoners of war to escape. They said they knew all about you being English and an enemy to Italy, and about how your husband had run away to aid the Partisans and left you to fend for yourselves here. They said you were all traitors."

"I knew that. We've always been suspect. But they searched the house and found nothing."

"Then they returned a second time."

"Yes. We're pretty sure we were betrayed by someone locally. A friend of my daughter Constanza's perhaps. Some careless talk…"

"It was I who told them, *Signora* Crivelli."

"You, Mario?"

"Yes, yes. I knew what you were doing, you see. My sister Maria, she would never betray you. She loves you all too dearly. But she's not very good at hiding things. It was not difficult to guess." He paused, wiped his face, then went on in a very low voice, "We co-operated. We told the Gestapo that you were hiding an Allied serviceman in your cellar and if they made a second search they would find him. We had to tell them – we *had* to! If it had been your boy wouldn't you have done the same? They would have tortured Renato to death. Killed him in the most horrible way. So we told them. And they stuck to their side of the bargain. Renato was released."

There was a long silence. In Rosemary's mind was the picture of what might have happened to Paolo on the night of the botched escape if he and Joe had been caught. Or to all of them if Joe's hiding place had been discovered. At last she said, "It seems we've all been forced to do a great many things we've hated doing, Mario. And I'm glad Renato's safe. That we're all safe, at least for the time being."

He took both her hands.

"Thank you, thank you, *Signora* Crivelli. I knew you would try to understand. And you won't tell Maria, will you? I couldn't bear her to know what we did."

"No, of course not. This will remain a secret between your family and mine, I promise."

"You are a true Christian, *Signora* Crivelli, a true Christian. *E una signora molto simpatica*."

He wrung both her hands and said goodbye. She watched him trudge off down the path towards his supper. Then she turned and walked slowly home.

"So it wasn't Hilaria who told them that second time," said Constanza. "I so hated her that day when she came to say goodbye, when the Albertinis were leaving for Como. But she'd come specially to warn us."

"Joe wouldn't have got away if she hadn't," Rosemary said. "And if he'd been found here…" She didn't go on. It was no use dwelling on that prospect.

The three of them were huddled together in Babbo's little study, which was now the only place in the house where they could be alone and have a little privacy. It was late and Maria had taken herself off to bed some time ago. The wireless operators were at work in the drawing room, but the rest of the house was relatively quiet.

"You two must never, ever, mention to anyone what Mario told me today," Rosemary told them. "It has to be forgotten. I know you're both old enough to understand that. Above all, Maria must never know."

"Of course, Mamma. We're not kids any more, you know. Though you sometimes seem to think so," said Paolo. Recovering his precious bicycle had gone a long way towards restoring his spirits. "All the same, I can't understand why you ever wanted Hilaria as a friend, Constanza. They're a terrible family. I was glad to see the back of them. Though there's a rumour in the village that Aldo, the Chinless Wonder, is still around in Florence. He's set himself up as a supplier of all sorts of stuff to the Allied Forces now – food, machine parts, toilet paper. Heaven knows where he's getting it from. But he's making himself so useful that everyone seems to have conveniently forgotten he was an out-and-out Fascist sympathizer, and probably still is."

"We can't hold Hilaria responsible for the things her brother does," said Rosemary. "She need never have bothered to come by that day. We owe her a great debt."

Constanza nodded her agreement. But she was in no mood to argue with Paolo. Since the day of Joe's departure she had been very quiet and withdrawn, sitting alone in her room, listening to her precious gramophone. Rosemary knew that she was finding Helmut's violent death very hard to get out of her mind too, and now there was this heart-sinking revelation about Mario. How was she going to resume life as a carefree teenager again?

Rosemary looked at her daughter's serious young face in the lamplight and thought, *When this war ends, it won't be a simple matter of defeat or victory.*

It will have spread its horrible, destructive tentacles out into all our lives long after the so-called peace has arrived. Heaven knows what sort of world Paolo and Constanza will have to cope with then. They've already had to grow up far too quickly. They've faced hunger, danger and death, yet there's been so little time for the ordinary teenage pleasures and rebellions, let alone a proper education. And I had so wanted it all to be different. Oh, Franco, Franco – when are you coming home?

CHAPTER 30

The army was moving on. Since dawn they had been clearing their tents from the garden, packing up equipment, loading stores onto trucks and dealing with vast amounts of refuse. To Maria's delight they were leaving some food behind: "Look, Paolo! English biscuits! Sugar! Tins of Spam!" They also left some storage jars, electric light bulbs, a whole set of shovels and, most precious of all, a tin-opener.

Captain Roberts shook hands warmly with all the family.

"You've been very patient, *Signora* Crivelli. I'm sorry we've been so much trouble."

"Not at all. It was the least we could do. A small

price to pay for being liberated, Captain. And we've been glad of your protection."

"I hope you'll have news of your husband soon. Perhaps some letters will start to come through. The railway's being repaired and restored as far as Arezzo, which is very good news. Our main thrust is north now, of course. We'll have a logistic base here in Florence, and we'll be supporting General Alexander's attack on Kesselring's Gothic Line. Won't be long before we're in Bologna!"

"I wish you the very best of luck, Captain."

The captain paused and looked up at the sky, which was a deep, cloudless, morning blue.

"Yours is such a beautiful country," he said. "I wish I could have seen it in happier circumstances. Do you know that I'd never been abroad until I was called up? Hardly been out of Guildford, except for the usual English seaside holidays. I'd seen pictures of Italy, of course, but it can't give you the feel of what it's really like – the hills, the buildings, this extraordinary light. I'm definitely planning to come back after this show's over."

"And when you do, I hope you'll visit us."

"I most certainly will."

His driver was waiting. He saluted, jumped into the jeep and was driven off.

After every last truck had departed, the house and garden seemed unnaturally quiet. Everything was in a sorry state. Cleaning up was going to take a depressingly long time and was such an exhausting prospect that Rosemary couldn't bring herself to think about it yet. Instead, she wandered about aimlessly in the garden, wondering how they would ever get around to filling up the shell hole or repair the damage that the tents had made to the grass. At the front gate she met the postman. She hadn't seen him for weeks and greeted him with great delight. He had brought one letter. She took it eagerly, hoping to see Franco's handwriting. But it was addressed to Constanza. The postmark was English and the handwriting unfamiliar. Constanza came running when Rosemary called her and took the letter. She didn't open it, but turned it over in her hands, looking at it. Then, without a word, she took it up to her room.

Rosemary was left alone by the front door. She knew she should be delighted that things were returning to some sort of normality and that Constanza had her letter. But for the first time in weeks she began to cry. They weren't tears of jealousy, just bitter, bitter disappointment. She wondered how much longer she would have to go on being supportive, kind and brave without anyone to turn to. She could cope with danger on her own, she knew that now. She could think fast under pressure and make lightning decisions when it came to protecting her family. But this long drag of loneliness and uncertainty, of never having anyone to lean on, to grumble to or confide in, was worse. It was shrivelling her up. *Perhaps Franco's dead,* she thought. *Perhaps I'll never see him again.*

Once she was upstairs, alone in her room, Constanza opened her letter.

"Dear Constanza," she read. This was crossed out and replaced by: "Darling."

I warned you that I'm not much good at writing letters. But this is to tell you that I'm OK. After we said goodbye that day I met up with some of our boys and now I've rejoined my unit. I'll never forget what you and your family did for me – your mom,

Paolo and especially you. I owe my life to you, you know that. Thank you just isn't big enough for what I'd like to say, but I hope I'll get the chance to tell you in person one day.

I am stationed in Britain now. Can't tell you where, of course. We'll be going over to Normandy soon, backing up the offensive there, and after that on to Berlin. To try to finish things once and for all.

Guess who I met in the Overseas Services Club? David! Seems that guy and I are destined to keep meeting up. He told me how he managed to escape with some other prisoners of war when the truck they were in was hijacked by the Partisans. Another local family put their lives on the line to hide him in their barn. In the end they got him back into Allied-occupied territory and onto a boat home. He won't be flying for a while. He's training other pilots. And guess what – he's getting married! Some guys have all the luck.

I think of you all the time. Dream about

you, too. I guess I've got nothing to offer but dreams right now. But I long for the day when I see your lovely eyes again and your smile. Can't wait to see you wearing that dress, to dance with you, to hold you in my arms.

Write me.

All my love,

Joe

Constanza read the letter through three times, folded it carefully and hugged it to her. Then she wound up her gramophone and put on a record: "J'attendrai".

Around lunchtime she was still sitting by the open window, her mind drifting far away with the romantic music, when she heard the sound of a car drawing up in the drive below. Two men got out but she couldn't see who they were. *I hope our house isn't going to be commandeered by the military again, when we've only just got rid of the last lot,* she thought. But who else could possibly have the use of a car when petrol was so scarce? She peered further out. There was only the one car – no jeeps or trucks. She heard voices, her mother's among them, then silence. Whoever had arrived seemed to have gone through to the back of the house. She waited for a call from downstairs but nothing happened, so she put on another record.

And then Maria burst into her room. "Constanza! *Carissima!* Come down at once – come quickly!" she urged.

Rosemary was standing on the veranda with two men. One was a stranger in uniform. The other was her father. He was bearded and thinner, and his face was more deeply lined than Constanza remembered it. He turned to her, radiant with joy at seeing her. For a few seconds she stood just looking at him. She found that she couldn't run towards him, not just yet. The shock of seeing him again was too great. And in his old way, realizing at once what she must be feeling, he simply grinned at her and said, "Constanza – my dearest girl – my darling one, I suppose now you're too grown-up to be told how lovely you've become since I went away."

Only then did she walk slowly towards him and bury her head in his shoulder. She wasn't crying but when she touched his face she could feel that his cheeks were wet. He held her close with one arm, the other was wound tightly around Rosemary's waist, as though never – even for a moment – could he bear to let either of them go.

The other man, clearly embarrassed at being embroiled in this emotional reunion, cleared his throat a little and stood at a distance, pretending to admire the ruined garden. Later, as they sat together over a glass of wine, he was properly introduced to Constanza as Colonel Fergusson. It was he who began to explain something of what Franco had been doing during his long absence from home: how he had been parachuted into Nazi-occupied northern Italy as a liaison officer and interpreter to help promote links with the Partisan units who were helping the British before the capture of Florence. Franco sat silently throughout.

"I don't have to tell you how dangerous it was," said Fergusson. "And especially courageous – as if he'd been captured by the Gestapo he would have had no official military status to protect him as a prisoner of war. Often he was acting as a courier for large sums of money that were being smuggled to the underground movement – and that made him particularly vulnerable. Several couriers disappeared

– their bodies were never found. Some were killed by local people for the money they were carrying; others were captured by the Nazis and were tortured before they were shot."

"I was lucky," said Franco, looking at his wife, who had gone very pale. "And I guess I was useful because I knew the area so well – every river and pass in the mountains up in the Mugello, from my old adventurous boyhood days. But it was so frustrating when I was working up there in secret, so close to Florence and so near to you all but not daring to get in contact in case I put you in danger. I was terribly homesick for you then. And worried sick when I heard the fighting was getting closer to you." He glanced at the crater the shell had made. "I can't bear to think that I wasn't here to protect you."

"We managed," was all Rosemary said. But then she added, "By the grace of God." She was holding her husband's hand very tightly. *I'll tell him all about it, bit by bit*, she thought. *Now, at last, maybe there will be time for us to be together, to get to know each other again.* She knew it wasn't going to be easy. She had been without him for so long. But slowly, like a warm patch of sunlight spreading and gaining strength, the wonderful realization that at last they were going to be a family again was dawning on her.

"Your husband is a brave man," Colonel Fergusson said when he took his leave. "He has risked his life over and over again to help the Allies in this area, and we're profoundly grateful."

"There were many others who did the same," said Franco. He was looking at Rosemary and Constanza. "And there are many different ways of being brave. But where's Paolo? Will he be back soon? I'm so longing to see him – my hero on a bicycle!"

Paolo was pushing his bicycle up the hill towards home. The need for lunch was drawing him back. He hoped there was something decent to eat for once. He had given up his night rides. Midnight sorties into the city were out of the question now, with all the bridges blown up and so many Allied military checkpoints around. And besides what had been a thrilling adventure earlier that summer seemed like kids' stuff after what he'd been through. Bike rides now simply offered a chance to be on his own, to try to get his thoughts in order. He felt his life was being held in some sort of limbo, free from immediate danger but still waiting for the real stuff to begin. He had no illusions about being a hero, on or off a bicycle. He had seen enough of war to know that he wanted no part in it. Well, not for the time being, anyway. He paused, realizing that he was in about the same place as he had been when he'd first encountered Il Volpe and his fellow Partisans. It seemed like a very long time ago.

When he arrived home he wheeled his bicycle to the shed, carefully avoiding Guido's old kennel. It made him sad to look at it. The house was very quiet. There seemed to be nobody about. He wandered around to the empty veranda, which looked out on to the pitted grass of the back garden. Over in the shade of the cypress trees his mother and Constanza were looking at the bomb crater with a man whom, for a moment, he didn't recognize. A bearded man, rather tall and gaunt. He had his arms around both of them. When he saw Paolo he disengaged himself and raised both his hands in a joyous salute.

Paolo stood still a moment, then took a few steps forward and then broke into a run.

"Babbo! Oh, Babbo! You're back!" he yelled, as he threw himself into his father's open arms.

Shirley Hughes has illustrated more than 200 children's books and is one of the best-loved writers for children. She has won the Kate Greenaway Medal twice and has been awarded an OBE for her distinguished service to children's literature. In 2007, *Dogger* was voted the UK's favourite Kate Greenaway Medal-winning book of all time. *Hero on a Bicycle* is Shirley's first novel.